The Kidnapping

MARY PETERSON

Copyright © 2019 Mary Peterson
All rights reserved
First Edition

PAGE PUBLISHING, INC.
New York, NY

First originally published by Page Publishing, Inc. 2019

ISBN 978-1-68456-975-5 (Paperback)
ISBN 978-1-68456-976-2 (Digital)

Printed in the United States of America

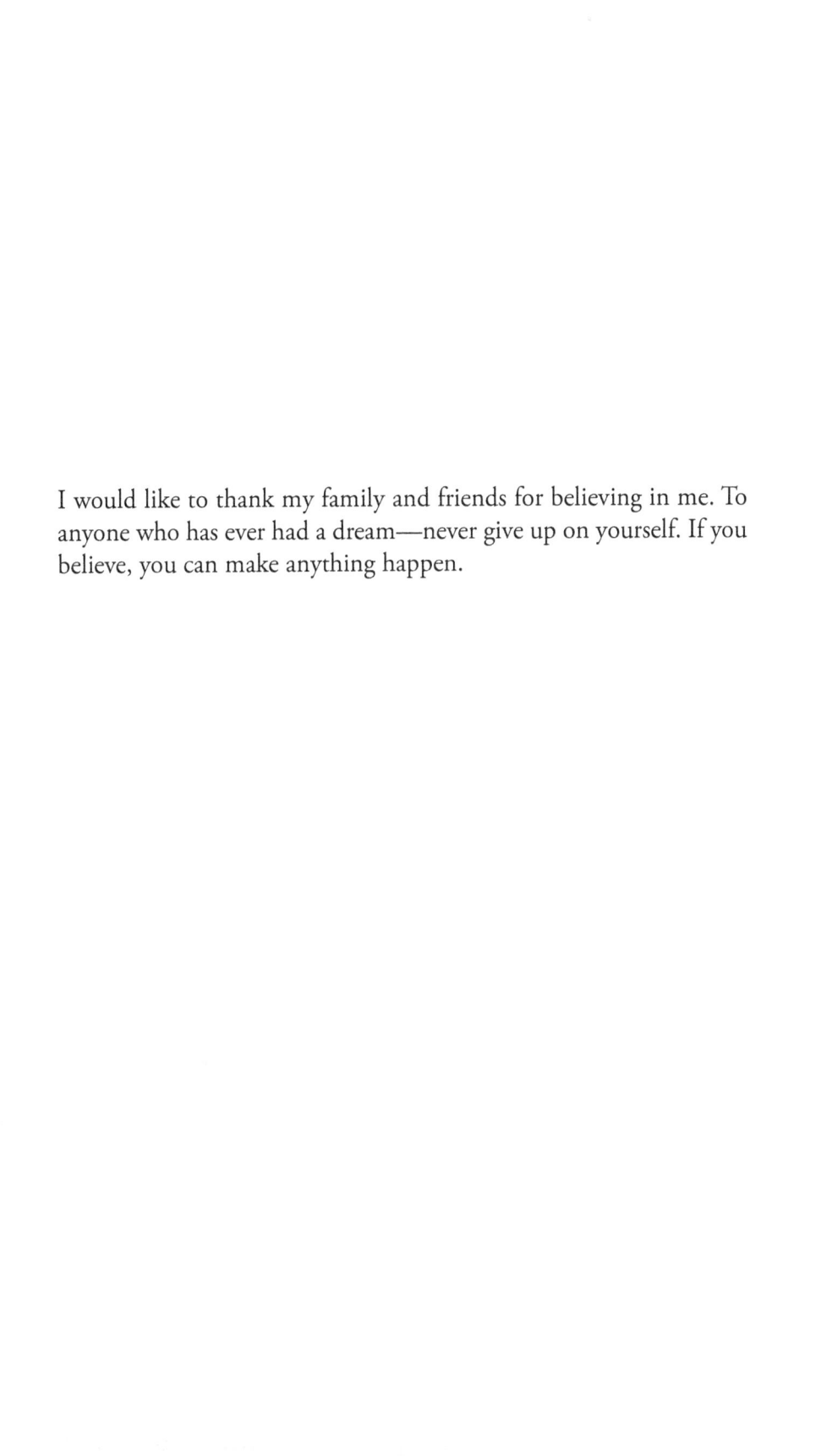

I would like to thank my family and friends for believing in me. To anyone who has ever had a dream—never give up on yourself. If you believe, you can make anything happen.

1

He was so hot! She wanted him to notice her but knew it would never happen. He was two years older and a senior in high school. Luke Jackson had blond hair and steely blue eyes. He was smart, athletic and didn't know she existed. They shared a class, and he sat two desks away from her. He was new to the school but didn't seem to have any trouble making friends, which was something that she struggled with on a daily basis. He was on the football team, and there were so many beautiful cheerleaders that she knew she didn't stand a chance. Plain, shy, and studious—that was her in a nutshell. Just once, she'd like to be the beautiful one that people would notice.

On her way home from school that day, a brand-new Mazda CX3 pulled up alongside her as she walked. The window was rolled down, and a male voice said, "Hey, do you need a lift?" At first, she ignored the question since no one ever asked to give her a ride home and then she dared to sneak a peek since the car didn't just drive away, and it was *him*. She couldn't believe it. Luke was asking her if he could give her a ride?! She was confused at first as to why he would ask her, and then she saw that there was another guy in the car. They started to laugh, and the car sped off. What a jerk! How could she be so stupid to think that anyone would be offering her a ride home, especially the hot new guy! She was so mad. Her eyes were stinging with tears so she hurried home. Once in the house, she slammed the door shut and ran up to her room. She was grateful that her mom was working; she didn't want to have to explain why she was upset. Since her mom and dad had gotten divorced, she felt like they were too intent on hurting each other to care how she felt about anything.

After doing her homework, she called her mom to see if she would be home for dinner. Her mom told her that sadly, no, she wouldn't since she was showing some homes in the area surrounding Paradise and probably wouldn't be home until dark. Sarah went to the kitchen and heated up some leftovers and ate in her room. She fell asleep before her mom got home and was awakened by her shoulder being shaken. She opened her eyes to see her mom standing over her looking irritated.

"Mom? What's wrong?"

Lynda said, "The front door was wide-open, how come?"

"I shut it when I came home from school and haven't been out since then. I did my homework, had something to eat, and must have fallen asleep." Her mom looked worried but didn't say anything else about it.

Lynda went back downstairs to see if anything was missing in the house and found it to be just as it had been this morning when she left for work. Thankful yet confused, she locked up everything and went up to take a shower before bed. These long hours were killing her, but she had to make a living for her and her daughter now that she was divorced from Glenn. They had been happy once—laughing, sharing, loving, and bringing an amazing daughter into the world. Together for sixteen years before he decided he was going to leave them for another woman. He'd been having an affair with Naomi for four years, and Lynda never knew it. He didn't work late, didn't go out alone, and had no expenses that would have pointed her in the direction of an affair. She had been devastated! Learning that her husband didn't love her anymore, was willing to throw away their life together, and leave her to raise their daughter alone left a very sour taste in her mouth. She currently didn't date and really had no desire to. They'd been divorced for a little over a year, and it still stung to think about it. Whenever they were near each other, they argued. It was all an ugly mess, and she really needed to stop being so angry for the sake of their daughter. Sarah was becoming withdrawn and very unsocial. She tried to talk to her about things, but Sarah was so closed off that she was getting really worried. Lynda thought to herself, *I need to take some time off so that we can go on a little get-*

away. When she was finished with her shower and got into bed, she resolved to take some time off to spend with Sarah.

The next morning, Lynda got up early and made breakfast for the two of them, waking Sarah up with the amazing smell of bacon and waffles. Sarah hurried to get ready so she could eat before school.

When Sarah sat down at the table, her mom said, "I'm going to take some time off so we can go on a little trip."

"Really? Where are we going?" Sarah asked.

"I was thinking we could go to the mountains and go skiing for a weekend. Would you like that?"

"Yeah, that sounds ok."

"Don't get too excited about it."

"It's just that we used to do that with dad and he won't be coming now."

"Ok, let's think of something that just the two of us can do, and we'll do that. I've got to run. Have a great day, honey. Love you."

Sarah got up from the table carrying their dishes to the dishwasher and said, "Love you too." Lynda thought to herself, *I have to come up with something great so that I can see that sparkle in her eyes again.*

2

Sarah was a little nervous going to school that day and had even thought about skipping but knew that they would call her mom, and she didn't want to deal with all of that. When it came time for algebra class, she was dreading seeing Luke. She was sitting at her desk when he walked in. She happened to look up, and her face got beet red. He looked at her, smiled, and winked. What was that all about? Maybe he's trying to make up for being a jerk yesterday, but she was still upset. Class was underway, and the teacher had his back to the room when a note was tossed onto her desk. She looked up, but no one was looking at her, so she was unsure of who may have thrown it. She opened it to see, "I'm really sorry about yesterday, Matt made me do it." She wrote back on it, "Do you always do what someone else tells you to?" and tossed it back to Luke. She wasn't really expecting a response and didn't get one. Once class was over, she went to her locker to get books for her next class when Luke stopped at her locker and said, "No, I don't always do what someone else tells me, but I wasn't sure how to start a conversation with you and Matt said he knew that you walked home from school and I could always see if you wanted a ride. I was so nervous; I started to laugh and had to drive off. Again, I'm sorry for being a jerk." Sarah was floored! Was he really here apologizing to her and telling her that he wanted to meet her. Why? *Why would this guy want to meet me? I'm nothing special.* And that's exactly what she asked him.

"Why would you want to meet me? I'm nothing special. There are a lot of beautiful girls in this school. Why don't you go talk to one of them?"

"I want to talk to you and get to know you," he stated.

"That trick you pulled yesterday wasn't cool, and I really don't want to talk to you so go find someone else to bother!" With that said, she stormed off to her next class. She was shocked at what she had just done but good for me! Once she finished her class, she was grabbing her books to take home with her to do homework when Luke stopped by again waving a white piece of paper.

"Truce?"

Sarah actually cracked a smile and said, "Maybe. It depends on how much of a jerk you decide to be."

"I won't be a jerk again! Can I drive you home today?"

"I'm not really sure that's a good idea."

"Why? I'll be a perfect gentleman."

"Well, if you promise to be nice, I'll let you drive me home."

"Scout's honor."

Sarah did smile at that, and they fell into step with each other heading to his car. He opened the door for her; she slid in, put her backpack on the floor, and buckled up.

Luke got in the other side, buckled up, and said, "Are you ready to go?"

Nervously, she answered, "Yes, thank you."

He laughed and said, "Hey, relax. I'm not a serial killer or anything. Do you want to go right home, or can we go to Ralph's?"

"I should get right home, my mom will be expecting me." Sarah knew her mom wouldn't be home for hours but didn't want him to know that she would be home alone.

"Ok. I'll take you home, but one of these days, you should come to Ralph's with me."

"Maybe I will, one day."

"Great! What's your address?" She told him and Luke said, "I have a favor to ask you." *Here it comes*, she thought. *he's going to want me to introduce him to some hot cheerleader.*

"What is that?"

"Would you tutor me in algebra?" his asked, face turning crimson.

"Really?"

"Yes. I'm not very good at it, and to be in sports, my parents said that I need to maintain at least a B average. I'm not getting a B in algebra, more like a D. I really can't bring home a grade like that. My parents will take me off the team."

"Why are you asking me? There have to be fifty other people you can ask."

"I think you're smart! You always raise your hand with the answers, and you're almost always the first one done with the tests. It seems like it comes naturally to you, and I really need the help. C'mon, what do you say? Will you tutor me?"

"Well, I guess so. What don't you understand about it?"

"Everything!" He laughed.

"Ok, this might be a challenge." She smiled. Inside, she was so excited she couldn't believe her luck. *He actually wants to spend time with me? This is the most amazing day ever!* "Where do you want to study?" she asked.

"We can do it at my house, or your house if you're not comfortable going to mine."

She had already lied to him telling him that her mother was expecting her, so she said, "I can't today, but we can start tomorrow if you'd like."

"Are you sure?"

"Yes. Tomorrow would work out just fine. I'll clear it with my mom, and we should be able to do it at my house."

"Great. You're a life saver, Sarah! Thank you!"

"You're welcome. This is it, thanks for the lift!" She hurried and got out of the car and ran up to the door.

Luke called after her, "Thanks again, see you tomorrow."

She turned and waved as he drove off. Opening the door, she sank against it when it shut not believing her luck.

3

Did that really just happen? Did he really just ask her to tutor him? How is this possible? She couldn't think straight, she felt like she was walking on a cloud.

She heard her mother call to her, "Sarah, is that you? How did you get home from school so quickly?"

Oh man, Mom really is home. "Hi, it's me!" she said as she walked into the kitchen. "I got a ride from a guy that I'm going to tutor in algebra. Is it ok if we study here sometimes?"

"What guy? What's his name? Where does he live, and who are his parents?"

"Wow, Mom, third degree, really? His name is Luke Jackson. He's new to the School, a senior who's on the football team and needs to bring his grade up in algebra. I don't know his parents. I haven't met them. He just asked me to help him out today."

"I'll need to meet all of them before I let you do this, so you just tell him that he needs to come over to meet me prior to any of this starting. I might be overly protective, but it's for your own good. You don't know much about him, and I don't know him or his parents."

"Oh for crying out loud, Mom! I can't believe you're being like this! He's a really nice guy that just needs some help so his parents don't take him off of the football team. If they were rotten parents, they wouldn't care one bit!"

"Just tell him I need to meet them! Why do you have to make everything so difficult, Sarah?"

"Because you're being ridiculous, Mother! I guess I just won't help him if you're going to be like this." And Sarah stormed up the stairs to her room and slammed the door. *Oh boy*, thought Lynda, *am I being too old fashioned? He's in high school but older than her, I don't know his parents and I don't know him. No, I'm doing the right thing. He may just have to find someone else to help him out.*

The next morning, Sarah didn't speak to her mother when she got up and got ready for school. Lynda tried to talk to her, but Sarah wouldn't answer her at all. She even offered her a ride to school and was ignored. Lynda thought, *she'll get over it*. Sarah left for school without a goodbye.

Once at school, she was hoping she wouldn't run into Luke, but he showed up at her locker and said, "Good morning, Sarah! I hope you had a nice evening. I told my parents I found a tutor to help me in algebra, and they would like to meet you and your mom if that's ok."

"They want to meet me? And my mom? What is it with parents? My mom said the same thing. She wants to meet you and your parents. When would be a good time for all of us to get together?"

"I can ask my folks what they have open this weekend and let you know. Would you give me your phone number, and I can call you tonight to let you know what they say?"

"You want my number?"

"Yeah. How else are we going to set up a time for us all to meet?"

"Um, yeah, Ok, it's 530-555-5309—that's our house number."

"Do you have a cell?"

"Of course I do, but I'm sure my mom would have a fit if I gave that out to you before she met you and your parents."

"Oh, I guess so. Ok, I'll check with my parents and call to see when you and your mom can meet us."

"Ok, sounds good. Sure am glad it's Thursday, then we can all get together and get this tutoring started for you."

"Me too. See you in class later."

"See ya."

Unbelievably, he just asked for her phone number, and she, like a dummy, didn't give it to him! Maybe she'll surprise him and give it to him in class later on, she'd have to think about it and see. Algebra

THE KIDNAPPING

was soon becoming one of her favorite classes only because she would see Luke. She walked in and there he was, talking to Stella, one of the prettiest cheerleaders in school. He looked up, saw her, and walked over to talk to her.

She sat down, and he said, "Hi, how's your day been so far?"

"Good, and yours?"

"Pretty good. I was thinking, what if you and your mom aren't home when I call tonight? I should at least have your cell so we can work this out with our parents."

"Oh, ok. I'll give it to you. 530-555-4138."

"Great, thanks! I'll drive you home again today if you'd like?"

"I would like that but won't Stella be upset?" He looked over at Stella, who was glaring at Sarah but, when she noticed that Luke was looking at her, gave him her most seductive smile.

"Who cares? She was asking me about something, I don't even remember. I'll meet you at your locker."

"Ok," she said, elated that there was nothing going on with him and Stella.

After school, they rode to her house and talked all the way. Getting to know each other, sharing a few laughs, and when it was time for her to get out of the car, she was a little sad but knew she would see him tomorrow and that he would be calling her to set up a time for their parents to get together. When she went in the house, she was alone, her mom still working.

She called her mom and said when she answered, "Mom, I'm sorry for getting upset with you about wanting to meet Luke's parents. They want to meet us as well. Luke will call after he's talked to his parents to see when we can all meet. What is your schedule like this weekend?"

"Oh, Sarah, honey, I'm so glad you called. I have several showings on Saturday but will be home after 3:00 p.m., and I'm free on Sunday before noon. I'm glad that they want to meet us. Now you know it's not just your old mom trying to be a pain. I have to run, sweetie. Love you!"

"Love you, too, Mom!"

Having cleared the air with her mom, Sarah felt better than she had all day, except when she was with Luke. She started on her homework and made a pizza happy the day had gone so well.

Luke called the house about 7:30 p.m. after practice. They talked about meeting up Saturday and where they wanted to go. They solidified their plans as Lynda was walking in the door and said their goodbyes. When they hung up, Luke thought to himself, *my plan is working!*

4

Fridays are usually the best day of the week and normally Sarah was supposed to go spend weekends with her dad. Pep rallies, football games, and hanging out with friends. Sarah did none of that. She barely had friends and as always, stayed home on a Friday night. She was watching a movie, since her dad had canceled on her yet again, when her cell rang. She didn't recognize the number, so she wasn't going to answer it, then remembered that she had given it Luke. *Oh well,* she thought, *there was a game tonight. I'm sure it's not him. He's probably out having a blast with his friends after the game.* Lynda came home about fifteen minutes later, and she finished watching the movie with Sarah. Although Sarah checked her phone like every two minutes, the mystery number never left a voice mail. Probably a wrong number.

Luke didn't leave a voice mail, but he decided to go over to her house to find out why she didn't come to the game. He got there, noticed lights on, and went up and knocked on the door. Lynda went to the door, looked out, and didn't recognize the man outside.

She said through the door, "May I help you?"

"Mrs. Wheeler? Hi, it's Luke Jackson, is Sarah home?"

Lynda opened the door and said, "It's very nice to meet you, Luke. Yes, Sarah is here. Let me get her for you." She walked to the living room where she had left Sarah, but she wasn't there. She called out to her, "Sarah, Luke is here to see you."

"What? I'm in the shower," she called back. Lynda went to the bathroom door, knocked, and went in.

"Sarah, why are you taking a shower now? We were going to watch another movie. Luke is here, and he wants to see you."

"Tell him I'll see him tomorrow, please Mom? I don't want to see him right now."

"Ok. I'll tell him we'll both see him when we all meet for a bite to eat. Oh, you never did tell me how good-looking he is either," she whispered.

Luke was still standing at the door when Lynda told him that Sarah was in the shower and that they would see him and his parents tomorrow. *Nuts,* Luke thought. *I'll call her cell again later. Maybe she'll answer. If not, I'll leave her a message this time.* Sarah finished up in the shower, relieved that Luke was no longer there. He made her so nervous it must be because he's popular and so good-looking. She still didn't understand why he'd want anything to do with her.

Her cell rang about 10:00 p.m., and she noticed it was the same number as before, but she still didn't answer it. The ringing stopped and then there was a beep. Someone had left a voice mail this time. She listened to the message and was thrilled that it was Luke. He had called to see if she was feeling ok. Since she didn't go to the game, he thought she might be ill. *He doesn't know that I had no one to go with,* she thought, and she wasn't going to be the one to tell him. She decided not to call him back because she didn't want him to think she was interested. *Damn! She didn't answer again. What is with her?* Luke contemplated. *Why won't she call me back? I know she's shy, but this is ridiculous! Why won't she talk to me? How am I going to get her to fall in love with me if she won't even answer her phone?*

5

Saturday morning chores were finished up, and Sarah was going to take a shower. Her cell rang again, it was Luke. *Wow, what is so important that he can't wait to tell me later on?*

She answered the phone, and he said, "Hey, Sarah! How come you didn't come to the game? Weren't you feeling well? Why don't you answer your phone? I called twice yesterday, but no answer."

"I didn't feel like going to the game. I don't typically answer my phone if I don't recognize the number. Sorry, it's what both of my parents have always told me. How did you know I wasn't at the game?"

"I was looking for you to see if you wanted to hang out afterward."

"Why? I thought this was a tutoring thing not spending time together outside of that."

"Well, ok, if that's the way you want it, that's cool. I have been enjoying getting to know you and thought we would have fun together. My mistake, sorry," and with that, Luke hung up.

"Hello?" No reply. Sarah felt awful!

Oh crap, he actually wants to get to know me better?! It's a miracle! At 3:00 p.m., Sarah was waiting for her mom to get home from work when the doorbell rang. Sarah wasn't expecting anyone and thought, *maybe Mom forgot her key.* She opened the door to find Stella standing there.

"*Bitch*!" Stella yelled at her and slapped her across the face. Sarah screamed, backed into the house, and slammed the door. Stella was already running away. Lynda got home about five minutes later to find Sarah with a red handprint on her right cheek.

"Oh my God, Sarah. What happened to you?"

"This cheerleader Stella came over, and when I opened the door, she slapped me and yelled bitch at me."

"But why? What did you do?"

"I didn't do anything except open the door," she exclaimed.

"Are you ok? Let me look at it. It doesn't look like she broke the skin; it's going to be red for a little while though. Put some ice on it until we leave."

Sarah went and got some ice and put it on her cheek. She really didn't want to meet Luke's parents with a red hand print on her face, so she hoped the ice did a little something to hide it. Maybe a little cover-up to hide the redness would be in order as well. As she sat there with the ice on her cheek, she racked her brain trying to figure out why Stella would do something like that to her. She didn't even know her or talk to her. Why would she be so angry and try to hurt her? Then it dawned on her, Luke! He had come over and talked to her and left Stella just standing there. That had to be it. *Stella was jealous of me!* she thought. *How ironic that a beautiful cheerleader would be jealous of me!* Crazy, she'd never have a boyfriend like Luke. That wasn't how the world worked. The plain, uninteresting girls never got the great-looking, popular boys. Stella didn't have anything to worry about, and she had half a mind to tell her so but decided to just leave it alone.

About twenty minutes later, they were ready to go. Lynda asked Sarah if she wanted to drive.

"You have to practice to get your license next summer," she said to Sarah.

"Ok. I'll drive as long as I don't have to parallel park. No one wants to see that" she said laughing.

They got into the car and went to the Black Bear Diner to meet Luke and his parents. Once inside, they let the hostess know they were waiting for three others and she informed them that they may already be there and led them to a table around the corner and they were sitting there waiting for them. Sarah's heart did a little skip when she saw Luke. *Oh my*, she thought, *he's so hot!!* The guys stood when they came to the table and sat after the ladies did. Luke introduced his parents and Sarah introduced her mom. Luke's dad, Larry, asked Lynda what she did for a living and she replied, "I sell real estate. I just started doing it about a year ago, and I enjoy it very much. How about you and Julia?" Larry said that he was an investment banker, and his wife was a private investigator. Sarah was wowed that Julia was a private investigator!

She asked her, "Do you love what you do? It must be so interesting to track people down, go on stake outs, and watch their every move. It just seems so exciting."

Julia laughed and said, "It isn't like what they show in the movies! It can be very long days with no progress at all. I work mainly with large corporations looking for fraud among their employees, so it isn't as glamorous as you think."

Lynda smiled and said, "I know what you mean! Selling real estate isn't always what it's cracked up to be either. Sometimes it takes everything you have not to walk out when someone nitpicks everything they see! It pays the bills though, so I'll keep trying for that million-dollar mansion to sell."

Luke and Sarah had been having their own conversation.

"Where do we want to start on your tutoring?" Sarah asked him.

Luke said, "At the beginning. I just don't get it! It makes no sense. Why would you put a letter in a math equation? What happened to just good old plus, minus, multiplication, and division? I know how to do that! I don't see when I'm ever going to use it anyway! It's dumb, and I shouldn't have to learn it!"

"Oh really?" said Julia. "I use it quite a bit in my line of work. There are always variables when you are working with more than one person! You don't know who, if anyone, is stealing or cheating, so you have to figure them all in to the equation and not leave anyone out. You'd be surprised how often you will find yourself using it, and I'm very happy that Sarah has decided that she can help you."

"I totally agree with you, Julia," Lynda confirmed. "I use it almost every day as well. I have to estimate how many people will show up for a showing and out of those people, how many may be interested enough to put in an offer and if more than one offer comes in I have to figure out if...well, you all know what I mean. Sorry to ramble. I'm glad that Sarah has agreed to help you as well. She's very patient and will do her best to make sure that you understand it."

Sarah blushed a bright crimson. Luke looked at her, smiled, and said, "I'm looking forward to someone helping me." They all ordered food and made light conversation while they waited for their meals. Larry looked at Sarah and asked her if she had her license yet.

"No, not yet, but I am practicing to get it this summer."

"Luke could probably take you driving. Tit for tat as we used to say. You teach him algebra, and he'll teach you to drive."

"Wow, Dad, that's a great idea! I never thought about that!"

"Oh, Mr. Jackson, that isn't necessary. My mom is teaching me."

"It seems like your mom is busy, and besides, if you are going to be studying, you can practice driving from your house to ours and back when Luke comes to pick you up for your sessions."

"Are you ok with this, Luke?"

"Sure I am. I think it will be fun to teach you how to drive. Do you know how to drive a stick?"

"I haven't a clue how to drive a stick. Maybe this isn't such a great idea after all."

"It will be fine. I'll show you how and then we can practice. We could even go to the school parking lot to practice on the weekends when there is no one there."

"If you think you can teach me, then I'm in."

"Wonderful! Now I don't feel so bad about you teaching me something and me having nothing to offer in return except my gratitude."

Their meals came, and they ate in companionable silence.

When the server brought the check over, Larry reached for it, and when Lynda tried to protest, he said, "Please let me do this. Your daughter was kind enough to agree to teach my son algebra, and it may not be that easy. This is my way of thanking her for taking time out of her schedule to help us, and I really appreciate it."

"That is very kind of you, Larry, thank you very much."

"Yes. Thank you, Mr. Jackson."

"Please, Sarah, call me Larry. I have a feeling we'll be seeing a lot of each other, and I don't want it to be so formal."

"Ok. Thank you, Mr.—er—Larry."

"It was so nice to meet everyone. Thank you for a lovely meal," Lynda said as they stood to leave. All the goodbyes were said, and Luke and Sarah made plans to start tutoring on Monday after practice.

6

The rest of the weekend was a blur. Lynda had gotten a request for another showing, and Sarah worked on a project for one of her classes. Monday morning, Sarah woke up feeling anxious. Not sure why she felt like this, she was getting ready for school and noticed that the redness on her cheek was fading. That's why, she would have to see Stella in algebra today, and she still didn't know why the girl had slapped her. She had her suspicions but wasn't sure. She decided that she would just let it go. She didn't want any trouble and wouldn't confront the girl. She just wanted to move on and not worry about it. Luke showed up at her locker that morning and noticed the slight redness on her cheek.

"What happened to your face?"

"What's wrong with my face?"

"It's red like you bumped it or something."

"Oh that. It's nothing."

"Sarah, it's a little red. Did your mom hit you?"

"*What?* No, my mom doesn't hit me. Just drop it, ok?"

"No, I won't. Who did that to you? Did you see your dad? Did he do this?"

"No, I didn't see my dad. It's really nothing. Please just let it go."

"I won't let it go until you tell me."

Frustrated, Sarah blurted out, "It was Stella. She came over to my house on Saturday before we were going to meet you and slapped me and called me a bitch. There, are you happy now?"

"No, I'm not happy! Why would she do that?"

"How do I know? Maybe it has something to do with the fact that on Friday, you left her standing there and came over to talk to me."

"No, do you really think so?"

"I don't know what to think. I just know that I am going to avoid her like the plague!"

"You don't need to do that. I'll take care of it."

"*No*! Luke, stay out of it. I don't like confrontation, and I don't want to deal with it! Please just leave it alone."

"Maybe. Hey, I'll see you in algebra."

With that, Luke walked off to class leaving Sarah there wondering if she had to worry about being slapped again because he wouldn't keep his mouth shut.

Sarah entered the classroom, and Stella started laughing and pointing at Sarah when she walked in. Embarrassed, she took her seat and opened her book. Stella started to make her way over to Sarah when Luke walked in and gave her a nasty look that stopped her in her tracks. She turned around and took her seat.

He looked at Sarah and said, "Hey, how's your day been?"

"Pretty good, you?"

"It's been ok. Not looking forward to this class but maybe I will once you teach me how to do it," he said and winked at her.

"Let's hope so," she said.

After class, Luke said, "I'll drive you home tonight and then come and pick you up after practice. Is that ok with you?"

"Yes. That should give me time to do my own homework before we work on your algebra."

"Great! I'll see you later."

"See ya."

Sarah was walking to her next class when Stella approached her from the opposite direction. "Bitch, have to have a guy fight your fights for you?"

"I don't want any trouble, Stella. I don't even know why you're mad at me."

"Luke is going to be my boyfriend, and you can't stop it! Look at you and your mousy hair and hand-me-down clothes! You're not popular or pretty and neither is your mother! No wonder your dad divorced her and left you both! You don't deserve to be happy!"

She laughed cruelly and walked off with her clan of followers laughing all the way. Sarah's face was burning red, and her eyes were welling up with tears. She turned, fled down the hall, out the door, and ran all the way home. She threw open the door, slammed it shut, ran up to her room, threw herself on her bed, and began to sob. She cried herself to sleep.

She was awoken but couldn't put her finger on what woke her up. Muffled sounds like someone was in the house. *Mom must be home*, she thought. Then she heard something break. Her heart started to pound, and she got scared. She grabbed her cell and crept to her closet. She hid behind some clothes and things in the closet and called her mom, no answer. She tried her dad, no answer. There were noises on the lower level, more things breaking, and she grew increasingly fearful! With no one else to call, she called Luke.

He answered on the first ring and said, "Where are you? I thought I was bringing you home after school? What happened?"

"Luke, not now!" she whispered. "Someone is in my house, and it's not my mom. Can you please come over here? I'm going to call the police."

"I'll be right there!"

Sarah called 911 and alerted the police that someone was in the house but not knowing anything else. She stayed on the line with them and, within a few minutes, could hear the sirens. The intruder must have heard them as well because the next thing she heard was a door slam. *Oh thank goodness*, she thought, *they've left*. She heard a scream just then and wondered what could be going on but was too afraid to leave her hiding spot. Seconds later, she heard, "Sarah. Sarah, are you all right?" It was her mom. Oh, thank God she hadn't been home when this happened, and she was ok. She left her closet, rushed downstairs, and threw herself at her mom giving her a hug. "I was so scared, Mom! I thought it might have been you, but you don't typically break things."

7

The police had arrived and had seen the person running away from the house. They gave chase and caught the intruder on the next block. One of the officers, Officer Hastings, came in to say that they had the culprit and that this shouldn't happen anymore. He advised them to lock their doors and windows. Luke came charging up the sidewalk just then and asked Sarah if she was all right. "I'm ok. A little shaky but ok." He enveloped her in a hug, taking her by surprise. It was a good surprise, and she held on.

"I'm sorry," she said to Luke.

"Don't be, I'm here."

She felt very comforted by this. She gave the police a statement even though she didn't know much only what she heard. Lynda asked the police if they knew the person who had come into their house.

"Yes. It's Stella Bergh."

"What?" both Luke and Sarah said together.

"But why?" she asked.

"We aren't sure. When we caught up to her and asked her why, she said, 'The bitch deserves it.' And that was all that she said."

Luke was fuming and demanded, "Let me talk to her. I'll get the answer out of her!"

"I'm afraid we can't do that, son. We'll take it from here."

The police left and Sarah, her mom and Luke all went inside. Lynda went around looking for missing items. All she found were broken pictures. Most of the family photos that Sarah was in had the glass broken out of the frame, and the photos were ripped. Luke and Sarah went to the kitchen and got a glass of water.

Sarah was shaking and Luke took her hands in his and asked, "Do you know why she would do this?"

"No. Unless she's mad because I'm going to tutor you. She came up to me in the hall at school today and told me that I didn't deserve to be happy and that you were going to be her boyfriend. I don't know what my tutoring you has to do with anything. It's not like we're dating or anything. Like I even stand a chance." This last statement was muttered under her breath, but Luke still heard it.

"Sarah, you are way too hard on yourself! Look, I like you, and I'm glad that we will be spending more time together so I can get to know you better. I'm just really sorry that she is being like this! I have no interest in her at all!"

Sarah looked at him is disbelief. *He* likes *me? He* wants *to get to know me?* She was over-the-moon happy! *I never thought that a good-looking guy would ever be interested in me! I just wish I was prettier! I wish I had better clothes!* Her face reddened, and he smiled and said, "I really like it when you blush. You look so cute!" *What is happening? Has the world gone mad? I'm not cute, I'm not pretty, and I'm not anything but a shy, quiet girl who wants none of the hassles that go along with boys especially if it's anything like what happened here today. No, thanks!*

She looked at Luke and said, "I really don't think I want to start tutoring this evening. Can we start tomorrow?"

"That's all you have to say? What's wrong, Sarah? I thought you'd like that I want to get to know you, that I think you're cute. I thought you liked me too," he said, looking hurt.

"Well, I don't. This is just a tutoring thing like you teaching me to drive. You're tutoring me as well." Inside, she was crying, *I do like you. I think I love you, but I can't tell you that!*

"Oh, ok, if that's how you want it, then that's what it is."

"One thing though, Luke, could you tell the other crazy girls that you and I are only working together to bring your grades up and that we are not an item now, and we never will be, please?"

"If that's really the way you feel, I'll stop bothering you. One question though, how come you called me tonight? Why didn't you call your mom or dad?"

THE KIDNAPPING

"I did, neither of them answered. I called you because, well, you are the only other person I could think of to call. I don't have many friends."

He knew she was a loner, and that's why he liked her. No one misses the ones that have no friends. He had to do whatever he could to make her fall in love him. *Maybe I better lay off for a little bit though. When we are alone at my house or driving, I can work on her. She* will *be mine.*

Sarah was dying inside. It hurt so much to say those things to him! She wanted to get to know him, she wanted to be around him, she liked him, might be falling for him, and she told him the complete opposite. She thought it was better than having the backlash of others trying to ruin her happiness. *Maybe Stella was right and I don't deserve to be happy.* She knew she didn't want to deal with bullshit from other girls, so this was going to be easier in the long run. Bruises and red spots healed, and so would her heart. She was going to have to try to make sure that this stayed more like a business proposition than anything else. She didn't know how that was going to work, but she was going to give it her best shot!

They had been working together for about two weeks, and Luke was grasping the concept of algebra better and Sarah was beginning to learn how to drive a stick. While Sarah kept putting Luke off, he kept trying to win her over. He was getting frustrated, and she was getting tired of trying so hard to pretend she didn't like him.

One day, he looked at her and said, "That's it, I've had enough! You and I are going on a date this Saturday night, and I won't take no for an answer. You won't come to a game to see me play, so I'm going to take you out, and we can be like normal people."

To her surprise and his, she said, "Ok. I would like that."

"Really?"

"Really. I was scared after the break in, and you came to help me. I really appreciated that. I will go out to eat with you but no strings attached."

"No strings," he agreed. "Fine, what time should I be ready?" she asked.

"Seven o'clock should work. We'll go to Mountain Mike's for a pizza and then to the arcade for something different. Is that ok with you?"

"That's cool."

Luke dropped Sarah off at home after their lessons. Sarah ran up to the house and let herself in.

8

"Mom?" No answer. She had to find something to wear for Saturday. Maybe her mom would buy her a new shirt or a new pair of jeans. She went to her closet and, after rifling around in there, found nothing suitable. *Oh, why do I even care? It's no strings. I could wear the same stuff he's always seen me in.* The only problem with that was that she wanted to have something nice and new to wear. Just then, the door closed, and she heard her mom call out her name. "Up here," she called back. Lynda went to Sarah's room and asked her what she was doing.

"Oh, trying to find an outfit to wear for the date I have on Saturday."

"What? A date? Oh, honey, that's fantastic! With who? No, let me guess, Luke?"

Sarah's face reddened, and she said, "Yes, Luke. Oh, Mom, can we please go shopping for a new outfit for me?"

"Well, as a matter of fact, we can. I just landed a big deal and got a check for a recent sale, so we can go and get you a few new outfits. It's been a while since we've been able to do that, and I'm sorry, honey!"

"No big deal, mom!"

"It is. A sophomore shouldn't be wearing hand-me-downs. She should have her own new wardrobe, and that's what we're going to do: go get you a new wardrobe. C'mon, it's still early. We'll grab a bite and get some shopping done!"

"Seriously?" she asked excitedly. "Right now?"

"No time like the present!"

"Thanks, Mom!"

Lynda decided they should go to Chico since the mall was much bigger than anything they had in town, and there were so many more places for a young girl to find clothes. They spent the rest of the evening shopping, snacking, laughing, and having a great time together. Sarah picked out enough new clothes that she wouldn't have to wear the same thing twice in the same week. (*It's been a while since that's happened*, thought Lynda.) Sarah was a good kid and deserved to be happy, and she really did need new clothes. She loved to see the smile on her face when she wasn't so worried about things. Lynda even splurged and bought a few new dresses for herself for work.

"Now let's get this stuff home so you can try it all on."

"Ok!" She was beaming. "Mom, can I ask you another favor? Can I get my hair done? Maybe get it cut and colored?"

"Absolutely! It's time for you to get a haircut, and I'd love to see what they would like to add to your hair for color. I'll call in the morning and make you an appointment for tomorrow evening after school. Oh, honey, I'm so happy for you!"

"Thanks, Mom." Sarah was so excited about getting her hair done that she started looking online for ideas as soon as she got home. She fell asleep with visions floating through her mind on what her hair would look like and how great she would feel when it was done.

She woke the next morning feeling light as a feather and practically floated down to the kitchen. "Good morning, Mother! What a lovely day it is today!"

"My, aren't you in a good mood today? Doesn't have anything to do with our shopping trip and the prospect of your upcoming date, does it?" Lynda smiled wryly.

"Why, of course it does! I can't believe how incredibly excited I am to get my hair done. I think I picked out just the right color and cut too."

"I'll be home around 4:00 p.m. today to pick you up and take you to your appointment. It's a good thing it's Friday, he won't see the new you until you go out on Saturday and won't you look stunning!"

THE KIDNAPPING

"I sure hope you're right, Mom! Have a great day! Love you and thank you again for letting me do all of this!"

Lynda picked Sarah up after school and brought her in to get her hair done. Sarah showed her ideas to the stylist, and the stylist pulled up the virtual screen on the mirror with Sarah's head up there and showed her what she would like in the style that she had picked out. Sarah didn't love the look, so they tried a few others until she gasped, "This is the one!" The stylist agreed and so did her mom. The stylist got to work, and when she was done, Sarah couldn't believe her eyes. She looked better than the virtual picture. She looked like a completely different person. She was in awe and almost started to cry. She looked up to see her mom wiping a tear off her cheek.

"Sweetheart, you look amazing!"

"I do, don't I? I can't believe this is me. I don't even look like the same person! It's incredible! Thank you for making me look so different."

The stylist said, "It's not hard to make a beautiful girl look beautiful. You just need some confidence! You'll be turning all the boys' heads now!"

Sarah blushed and said, "I sure hope you're right. It would be the first time in my life that's ever happened."

They left the salon and went in search of food. They opted for a Chinese place since it was fast and on the way home. Lynda kept looking at Sarah and smiling and finally said, "I'm so proud of you! You took a chance and stepped out of your comfort zone. I know it wasn't easy, but how do you feel?"

"I actually feel really good. I guess I've just been afraid because no one has ever showed interest in me, and I thought no one ever would. I can't thank you enough, Mom. You've encouraged me to do this for a few years, and I should have listened to you before. I can't wait for Luke to see me. I don't think that he will even know who I am."

"Of course, he will! You're my beautiful daughter who just needed a little bit of incentive to want to update her look, that's all."

Just then, Sarah's phone rang, and it was her dad. She answered it excitedly as she hadn't talked to him in a while. "Dad! How are you? When are we going to get to spend some time together? I miss you." Lynda sat waiting for her to get off the phone and could see by Sarah's face that she wasn't getting good news from her father. Damn him! Why does he continue to break her heart? She could only hear Sarah's side of the conversation, and it didn't sound very promising that she was going to get to see him any time soon.

"Ok. Uh-huh. Oh. Well, ok. Bye, Dad."

"What is it, honey? What did your dad say?"

"He said that he's too busy making plans for the wedding to spend time with me right now but would like me to join them when they get married. I don't want to do that. I barely know the woman. Besides, he cheated on you with her. I don't want to be there when they get married!"

"Do you want me to call him and tell him that for you?"

"No. I'll think of something so I don't have to go." She brightened up and said, "Maybe I'll have another date when they get married, and I won't have to go."

"You should go and show your support to your father."

"But I don't support what he's doing, or that woman he plans on marrying."

"I know that, Sarah, but it would mean a lot to your dad, I'm sure."

"I don't care! He hasn't been around for me lately when I've needed him, has he? No, he hasn't! What did he say when the house was broken into? Start locking your doors? Get a dog? No. He said, 'Well, shit happens. No use getting upset about it and move on.' That's not real supportive now, is it?"

"No, you're right, it wasn't. Maybe you'll feel differently when the wedding is closer. When are they getting married?"

"He said three weeks."

"Oh my, that's fast."

"Not really. They've been having an affair for how many years?" Lynda looked like she had been slapped. "Oh, Mom, I'm sorry, I didn't mean it like it sounded."

"It's ok. It's the truth. I was just too blind to see it right in front of me. Oh well, let's stop talking about this and tell me where Luke is taking you."

They talked about the plans that her and Luke had coming up and that made the conversation with her dad all but disappear. Once they got home with even more packages, they said their good nights and went to bed.

9

Sarah's phone rang about three in the morning. She didn't recognize the number, so she didn't answer it. She wondered who would be calling her so early. There was a beep alerting her that a message had been left. She looked at the caller ID again and then listened to the message. It was Stella calling to harass her. She thought that the police had told her that she wouldn't be bothering her again. *How in the world did she get my cell number?* she wondered. Her phone rang again about fifteen minutes later waking her up again. She looked, and it was a different number she didn't recognize. Again, she didn't answer and was left another message by Stella. *She must be with some of her clan calling and bothering me.* Sarah got a little scared but decided to turn off her phone so they wouldn't keep her up all night calling. When Sarah got up in the morning, there were fifteen missed calls and that many messages; all of them mean and hateful. She told her mom about it, and her mom said, "That's it. This is harassment and bullying. We're taking this to the police." They left for the police station after breakfast. Detective Hastings was on duty, and they let him listen to the messages.

He said, "Do you want to press charges? This is a form of stalking and bullying, and we don't take that lightly."

Lynda started to say yes, but Sarah interrupted saying, "No! I have to go to school with these girls. If you take her away, the others will be after me. My mom wanted you guys to know that this was happening, but I don't want to make waves. It may get me in more trouble, and I certainly don't need that!"

THE KIDNAPPING

They went back home and Lynda had to go to a showing. "I want you to lock up after I leave and don't open the door for anyone! Do you understand?"

"I'm not a baby, Mom. I can take care of myself."

"Just, please, lock the door? Is Luke coming to get you?"

"Yes, he'll be here at five."

"Ok. Have a fantastic time, honey!"

"I'll do my best. I just wish other people would leave me alone. I never did anything to them!"

"I know. We'll see if she continues this behavior. If she does, then I really think that we need to get a restraining order and/or press charges against her. You'll become a prisoner in your own home and that isn't healthy. You're just coming out of your shell. I don't want someone to put you back in it!"

"I don't want that either. I guess we'll have to wait and see what happens. Bye, Mom. I'll lock the door, I promise!"

"Goodbye, pumpkin. Have a great time!"

Lynda left, and as promised, Sarah locked the door. She was getting ready for her date when the doorbell rang. Sarah wasn't expecting anyone but Luke. She went to the door and asked who it was. "Bitch! Going to the police to tattle on me? Not the best move you've ever made! I'll be watching you, and when you least expect it, I'm coming after you!"

"*Go away, Stella!* I'll call the police right now if you don't leave!"

"Oh, I'm shaking. I'm so scared. *Not!* Don't you get it? Over my dead body will you have anything to do with Luke! I will make him mine, and I don't care who thinks they can stop me. They won't so just watch your back."

Sarah was shaking. She stepped away from the door, heard a car door slam, and went to the living room window and peeked out. She saw Stella laughing in the passenger seat of the car. She really wanted this to stop. She had to talk to Luke and let him know what Stella was saying. Maybe she *should* press charges. That might not be the best idea. If Stella had slapped her, what would her clan do to her if she had their ring leader arrested? She shuddered to think about it.

10

Luke arrived right on time. He walked up to the door and stopped short. *What the he…?* He called Sarah's cell to see if she was home. She answered but seemed disappointed that it was him.

He asked, "Are we still going out tonight?"

"I thought so, unless you're calling to cancel."

"No. I'm referring to what is attached to your door."

"What? What are you talking about?"

"Are you ok? This is very odd. Come out and take a look."

"Give me a minute. I'm almost ready." A minute later, Sarah opened the door to see Luke staring at her like he just saw a Cinderella. "What are you looking at me like that for?"

"Sarah, you look amazing! I love your hair. You look even more beautiful than before!"

Her face got bright red, and she said, "Thanks! You look pretty good yourself." He had on a blue shirt with a sport coat and nice slacks. "Now, why would you think that we wouldn't be going out tonight? What's on the door?"

He had taken the offensive item off the door and tossed it in the trash outside. He didn't want to show her but decided he better. He brought her to the garbage, flipped open the lid and when she peered inside, saw a Barbie doll covered in a red substance with the throat cut so the head was barely hanging on. She gasped and turned her face away.

"Who would do this?" Luke asked her.

"Stella. She was here earlier and threatened me and she called me about twenty times last night to tell me that you were going to be her boyfriend and she wasn't going to let anyone get in her way. I was trying to put it out of my mind, but if this is going to be what happens when I like a guy and want to go on a date, I can do without it!"

"You like me?"

"Well, yeah," she said shyly.

He smiled broadly and said, "Good, I like you too and I hated it being one-sided. I'm glad you told me about Stella. I'm going to put a stop to her bullshit once and for all!"

"Luke! No, you can't say anything to her. She'll come after me, and it will be way worse. The police want me to press charges for her stalking and bullying me, and this is good evidence. Let's call them now, and we can go out after, ok?"

"Promise? That we'll still go out after we talk to them?"

"Yes, silly, I promise."

They called the police, and once Detective Hastings arrived, they told him what had happened. He asked where the Barbie was, and they showed it to him in the trash. He explained that they should have left it where it was, but Luke said he wanted it off the door to try to spare Sarah the hassle. Detective Hastings said, "I understand, but it's still tampering with evidence." They showed him the red stuff on the door. No one was quite sure what it was. Sarah told the cop that she indeed wanted to press charges now as this was the last straw. "I need to call my mom and let her know what's happened." She called her mom and told her what happened, that she was pressing charges, and she and Luke were still going out. Hastings said he needed to call the Crime Scene Investigators (CSI), but they could leave if they wanted to since he had their statements. *Finally*, Luke thought, *we're free to go on our date.*

11

They went for pizza and then to the arcade, talking, laughing, and having a great time. Luke complimented her several times on her new hair and clothes, which just embarrassed Sarah, but she thanked him for noticing. It was getting close to curfew, so they headed back to Sarah's house. When they arrived, he got out, opened her door, and they walked up to the front door, which her mom had cleaned off thankfully, and Sarah shivered a little. Luke asked if she was cold, and she said no, just remembering what happened earlier. He put his arm around her and pulled her to him, and she sank into his arms, loving the feeling and thinking, *this feels nice!* He tilted her face up to his and kissed her. Gently, lovingly, sweetly, he kissed her. She saw fireworks! *This must be love*, she thought as she returned his kiss. It grew in intensity, and she responded.

"*Ugh*! I'll kill you! You *bitch!*" Stella came storming out of nowhere and tried to get to Sarah. Luke grabbed her and said, "What the hell is your problem? Sarah, call the police!"

"I want you for myself! You can't like someone like *her*! She isn't worth your time! I'm pretty and smart, and you should be with me!" Stella was sobbing and trying to get to Sarah still. Luke held onto her firmly, so she tried to put her arms around him and kiss him. He turned her away from him but continued to hold onto her, his face saying everything as he looked at her in disgust.

"Stop it, Stella! You and I will never be a thing! I don't like you. I don't even want to know you after everything you've done! What the hell is wrong with you? Who are you to say who I can and can't like? I like Sarah, and you're just going to have to live with it. Leave her alone, or I will make your life a living hell. I promise you that. Do you understand?"

"I will not. I will kill her before I let her have you!"

"Are you nuts, Stella? I have no feelings for you! You will not touch Sarah again. Are we clear?" Hearing sirens in the background, he told her, "Now you're going to jail, and I'm a witness to your special kind of crazy!"

Lynda had heard the commotion, so she opened the door to see what was happening.

She said, "What in God's name is happening out here?"

"It's Stella, Mom. She came out of nowhere and threatened me again. The police are on their way."

"What? Are you ok, sweetheart?"

"I'm fine, Mom. Thankfully Luke stopped her. I think she's really unstable."

The police arrived and took everyone's statement. Stella was hauled away in the back of the squad car, placed under arrest for stalking, attempted battery, bullying, and defamation of property. The officer told them that she admitted to being the one that had broken into the house when Sarah was sleeping and stolen the Barbie that was hung on the door earlier that day.

"What an incredibly long day it's been," Lynda stated. "You two can come in the house if you'd like. I'm going to head up to bed. Early day tomorrow for me."

"I'd better be going home. It is getting late, and I'm past my curfew."

"I could call your mom and dad, Luke and explain to them what happened."

"No, that's ok. I'll tell them all about it when I get home."

"Well, good night then, Luke. Thanks for taking care of my girl!"

"Good night, Lynda, it was my pleasure. I'm just glad I was here when this happened. Stella really is crazy." Lynda went back into the house, and Sarah and Luke were left alone again.

"Well, it is late, Luke, and I'm exhausted after this day and everything that has happened. Thank you for a great time."

"Where do you think you're going?"

"I'm going to go inside and go to bed. I'm beat."

"One kiss goodbye is all I ask before you leave me out in the cold," he said and winked at her.

She turned a nice shade of pink but gave him a kiss, a very short kiss and bolted into the house calling good night as she went in. Luke turned to go and was surprised at how much he had enjoyed this evening even with crazy Stella trying to ruin it.

Lynda was so excited when she got off the phone on Tuesday morning, she couldn't believe her luck! This new listing that just called was in a very affluent neighborhood in Chico and it was listed for 1.9 million dollars and she landed the call. She still needed to meet with them and put together a plan to sell their place, but she was ready for the challenge. She had gotten new clothes for just this occasion. You had to look the part if you wanted to sell the ritzy places. Her meeting was Friday morning, and she had a lot of work to do in that short amount of time to get ready and land this deal. Sarah was busy with Luke and things seemed to be calming down after the whole Stella thing, so she felt safe immersing herself in work. Besides, Sarah was supposed to be going to her dad's wedding this weekend. Even though she didn't want to go, she had asked Luke if he would go with her and he said that he would, so she felt better about going. Lynda was so very happy for her daughter, she found a nice young man who seemed to adore her, she came out of her shell and was blossoming into a beautiful young woman. Her future looked bright. Hell, both of their futures looked bright! If she could land this deal and close this sale, she would be able to pay off the house and buy a new car. They wouldn't be living paycheck to paycheck anymore and that was something she couldn't believe was right in her grasp. Lynda texted Sarah that she wouldn't be home much the next couple of days because of a potential new deal and left to get started on it. Sarah saw the text from her mom and texted her back, "Go mom!"

12

Friday after school, Sarah went up to her room, packed her bag, and thought for the millionth time that she should call her dad and tell him that she wouldn't be at this stupid wedding. Although Luke had agreed to go, she still didn't want to. They were going to stay at her dad's (in separate rooms, she assured her mother) and would be home sometime around dinner on Sunday. She was just finishing packing up when she heard a knock at the door. She went down to see who it was.

It was Julia, so she let her in. "Hi. What brings you by, Julia? Luke isn't here but should be here around 4:30 p.m.–5:00 p.m."

"Oh, I'm not here to see him, dear. I came for you."

"Really? What's going on? Is Luke ok?"

"Yes, he's just fine. I just thought it would be nice if you would come with me to the house so you and I can get to know one another a little bit better while we wait for Luke to come home from practice, ok?"

"Sure, I guess. Let me get my bag." She ran up the stairs, grabbed her bag, and left with Julia.

13

Lynda was so busy getting the comparables and everything ready for this new listing that when it came time for Sarah to be home, she barely realized what time it was. Just then, her stomach growled, reminding her that it was close to dinner. *Wonder where Sarah is*, she thought. *Maybe they stopped off for a bite.* She made a quick dinner and got back to work. Only a few more things left to do to call it good. Around 10:00 p.m., she looked at the clock and really wondered where Sarah was, it's way past dinnertime. She called her cell, and it went right to voice mail. *Hmm, maybe she forgot her charger, and her phone was dead.* She called Luke's cell, and he answered right away.

"Oh, hi, Luke. It's Lynda. Is Sarah there with you?"

"No. Why, isn't she there?"

"No. You guys were supposed to go to her father's this weekend for the wedding. Didn't you go?"

"No. She text and canceled on Friday. Said she thought about it, changed her mind, and wasn't feeling that great so she wanted to rest. I figured I'd see her at school on Monday. She really isn't there?"

"No, and now I'm worried. She isn't here, and her phone goes right to voice mail. Oh no, do you think any of those girls came over and took her or something?"

"I don't know. I can come over, and we can look around for her if you'd like?"

"I'll look and see if there is anything around here that will tell me where she went. I'll call you back if I find something. If you hear from her, please have her call me immediately."

"I sure will. Please let me know what you find."

"Ok."

Lynda was worried and decided to call her ex to see if Sarah just showed up on her own, not wanting to bring Luke after all. Glenn answered on the second ring.

"Lynda, what do you want?" he said tersely.

"Hello, Glenn," she responded coolly. "Is Sarah there? She was supposed to be going to your wedding with a boy she's been seeing, but he said that she canceled, and I'm hoping that she just decided to go on her own."

"She's not here, never showed up," he said angrily.

"I'm going to call the police. She was having some problems with some of the girls around here, and I need to find out if they did something to her."

"You mean she's really missing? Oh God, Lynda. What can I do?" *He actually sounded worried*, she thought.

"I won't know what to do until I talk to the police. As soon as I hear something, I'll let you know."

"Please keep me posted. I know we've had our differences, but she is my daughter, too, and I want to know that she's safe."

"Maybe if you'd bother to spend time with her, she would have gone to your wedding, and she wouldn't be missing right now. I have to call the police." She hung up without a goodbye. She called the police department and asked to talk to Detective Hastings.

She was put through, and he asked her, "How can I help you? Is Sarah all right, or are those girls still harassing her?"

"Oh, Detective Hastings, I don't know. She was supposed to go to her dad's with Luke Friday, and Luke said she canceled on him, but she isn't here, and her dad hasn't seen her. I've been swamped this weekend and didn't realize she was missing until now. I don't know what to do I have no idea where she is. Please, you have to help me!" She wailed.

"Wait, she's missing? I'll be right over. Call Luke and have him meet me at your house, then I can talk to both of you."

Lynda called Luke and asked him to please come over because Detective Hastings wanted to interview him as well. He said he'd be right there. When Luke arrived, he knocked on the door, and Lynda opened it with tears streaming down her face.

"Oh, Luke, where could she be?"

"Have you heard from her at all? What did her dad say?"

"I haven't heard anything, and he hasn't seen her. I called the police only because she's been having trouble with those girls. What exactly did she say when she canceled your plans?"

"She text me that she didn't want to go to the wedding with me and that she thinks we should stop seeing so much of each other. I was pissed when I read it, and I tried to find her to ask her what it was all about, but I couldn't find her. I came over here after practice Friday hoping she might change her mind, but there was no answer. She didn't answer the door, and she didn't answer her phone." Just then, Detective Hastings walked up to the house and knocked on the door.

"Officer, please come in."

"Ok, start at the beginning and tell me everything that you know." Luke started and told him what he had just told Lynda. Lynda said that she had worked all weekend and wasn't worried about Sarah because she was supposed to be out of town at her dad's wedding. She didn't get worried until she looked at the clock around 10:00 p.m. and realized they weren't back yet. "Well, have you gone through her room to see what is missing? What about anything else in the house? Is there anything missing?"

Lynda said, "I've been so worried, I never bothered to look. We can all go and look around if you'd like. Luke's been here enough that he might spot something missing too."

They all went in search of anything that might tell them where Sarah was. After searching the house, Lynda noticed that only two days' worth of clothes were gone. They were no closer to knowing where she might be then when they started.

Lynda started to cry, "Where is my little girl? What am I going to do? What if that girl Stella has her and is torturing her or has taken her somewhere and left her alone or has killed her? Oh my God, I can't take this!"

Detective Hastings said, "Lynda, it's not going to do you any good to get so worked up. You have to keep a level head if you're going to help find Sarah! Now, Luke, is there anything else that you can remember?"

Luke had been pretty quiet when they searched the house and stated, "No. I can't think of anything. All this time, I thought she was blowing me off because she didn't want me to meet her dad. Maybe the text she sent wasn't even from her."

Detective Hastings said to Luke quietly, "If you think of anything else, please let me know. I know Lynda is scared and worried, and I don't want you adding to that worry. If you remember anything, come to me before telling her."

"I will, Officer. I swear," he said as he left.

14

When Luke returned home, he went to his mother and asked her, "What have you done with Sarah?"

"I've got her in the fallout shelter. Why?"

"The police and her mom are looking for her. I think it's time that I find and save her. There are some girls at school that are being mean to her, and the police think they might have had something to do with this. Do you know Stella Bergh? She has been acting crazy saying that I'm going to be her boyfriend and that she is going to hurt anyone that gets in her way."

"I do know her and her mother, and I told Stella that you might like her. I only told her that because I don't think that Sarah is good enough for you. She's so drab and plain."

"She's perfect just the way she is. She likes me, and I like her. Now let's go and get her out of that room."

"Why don't we do this after school tomorrow? I'll go in there, give her a little bit more sedative, and she should be fine to rescue tomorrow. Ok?"

"As long as she is safe in there and isn't hurt, I guess that will be fine."

Luke went to school the next day fully expecting to see the police. He hung out with his friends at lunch and before school was out, one of them asked, "What happened to that chick you were seeing? She get wise and break up with you?"

"Actually, she's missing. We were supposed to go to her dad's wedding this weekend. She text me she didn't want to go and now she's missing."

"Aw c'mon, man. What'd you do with her?" Chuckles and snorts joking around.

"I didn't do anything with her. She's gone, and no one knows where she went."

"Seriously, man?"

"Yeah, seriously."

"Wow. Where do you think she is?"

"No idea, man. She just disappeared." Once Luke got back to home, he parked in the garage and went inside to talk to his mom. "I want Sarah out of that room right now!"

"Ok, let's go down and get her." They went down the stairs to the fallout shelter where his mom put her index finger on the pad, and the door slid open.

Luke walked in and said, "Where is she?"

"She should be here."

"Sarah? Where are you?" he called. There was no answer. He called again, "Sarah! Are you here?" He turned toward his mother, got in her face, and shouted, "Where is she? What have you done with her?"

"She should be here. I put her here Friday after school."

Julia looked concerned. She didn't want anything to happen to the girl, just wanted Luke to forget about her. She had planned on bribing the little hussy to stop seeing her son, but what could have happened to her? She and Larry were the only ones that could get into this room. But he left Friday, so he wouldn't even have known she was here unless he had come down here for something. He kept things in here she didn't want to know about. He was acting strangely on Friday before he left. Maybe he had spied on her or heard something from down here, but no, that can't be, this was a soundproof room. Luke grabbed his mom by the arm, and they checked the bathroom and under the bed, but there was no sign of her. Luke was getting angrier by the minute.

"Where is she, woman? You better tell me this instant, or so help me, I'll leave you down here to rot!"

"Luke, I swear I don't know where she is. She was here Friday, and I haven't been down here to check on her since. I did have a thought though, what if Larry found her and took her with him? I don't see her bag, so maybe he did find her."

"Why in the world would he do that?"

"Larry is a sick man, Luke. He has twisted sexual fantasies that I draw the line at and he goes away every so often to fulfill those fantasies and I'm ok with him going and doing that."

"After all the nasty men you've fucked, why would you finally draw a line? How bad could those fantasies really be?"

"I won't tell you anything about them, but if Larry has her, she will come back a changed person if she comes back at all."

"You make me sick! You said you were going to come down here last night and check on her. Why didn't you? I can't believe you! Why would you want to take her away from me? Why would you want to hurt me so much? I think you should stay down here for a few more days."

"Luke, you can't leave me down here. You can't get in the door, only Larry and I can."

"Then I guess you will be staying down here until he gets back from wherever he is. He better have Sarah with him when he comes back, or there will be hell to pay!" Luke stormed out of the shelter and hit the close button on the keypad while his mother looked at him and cried. "No please, Luke, don't leave me in here!" was what he heard as the door was closing.

Luke got home from practice the next afternoon and went down to check on his mother. He looked at the keypad and thought, *There has to be a way for me to gain access, they did it when we moved in.* He played around with it until he finally got to the point where he could add his print to the keypad for access. The door started to open, and Julia thought it must be Larry. "Oh thank God. Larry!" She got up and was going to go to the door when Luke walked in and said, "So, Mom, how does it feel to be all alone with no one worried about you? How would you like me to leave you down here until Sarah is found? Doesn't sound too great does it? No? Well, welcome to my world! I remember what you did to me when I was little. I know that your husband is not my real father, and we didn't always have money. I know what it's like to not be wanted, to feel like you're always in the way, to feel unloved. It's not easy sitting here with your thoughts is it? I was a little boy that thought his mother hated him. You would rather fuck those nasty-ass men than spend time with me. How could you do that to me? It's not fun is it, Mom? Where is she, Mother? What did you do with Sarah?"

She winced at the words he threw at her. She believed he may just be mad enough to kill her down here. She knew she hadn't been the best mother but had tried to make up for it when she met Larry. She thought she hit the big time and that Luke may have been too young to remember how she had put him in the basement when she had gentlemen callers. She had told him to be as quiet as he could and to not move. He had come up the stairs once and luckily she had seen him before the guy she was with did and was able to get him back downstairs. She had been high on drugs and alcohol and had actually forgotten him down there for a few days. She couldn't remember how many now, but he had been filthy. His smell had made her stomach turn. *I did that to him*, she thought and vowed that she would never do anything to hurt him again. She held true to that promise she made. She tried to make up for it for years, matter of fact, she thought she had. Until Friday evening when her world came crashing down around her. Her husband had left because he needed his time away. Now Luke was telling her that Larry still wasn't back, and she was getting worried that maybe Larry really did have Sarah. She was so lost in her own thoughts that she didn't hear Luke ask her a question.

"Mother, what happened to Sarah? Did you kill her and dump her somewhere so that I won't ever be happy again? Did you tell Larry to take her on his sick weekend and to not bring her back? *Where is she*? Tell me right now, or I'll kill you and leave you down here to rot!"

"*No*! Please, sweetheart, don't do this to me. I honestly don't know where she is. I'm sorry for everything that I ever did to you when you were little! I was trying to make money so we had a place to live. I was hoping that you wouldn't remember much of it. Please, take me out of here with you?!"

Luke thought about it for a minute and decided that it would be better if he could keep an eye on her. He would use her as bait for Larry to bring Sarah home, if he had her. If he didn't, where was she? He brought his mother upstairs so she could call Larry and find out if he had Sarah.

15

Larry couldn't believe his luck. Luke's girlfriend was in the fallout shelter when he went in to get some supplies for his trip! When he opened the door, there she was begging him to take her out of that room. He eagerly agreed if she promised to be quiet as a mouse while he snuck her out of the house. She agreed wholeheartedly and was quiet as a mouse. He told her to get in the car, and he'd take her home. She got in the car, tossed her bag on the floor at her feet. He offered her a bottle of water which she drank greedily. She thanked him over and over again for saving her then her words started to slur and she was out like a light. *Perfect*, he thought. Now she wouldn't be able to fight him when they didn't go to her house to bring her home.

Sarah didn't understand why she was locked in this room! How in the world was she going to get out? She tried to call someone on her cell, but there was no reception in this room. Why would Luke's mom want to keep her here? Did Luke know? Was he part of this? Was she in danger? Her head was swimming. She yelled and screamed, but no one came. She finally sat in the corner of the room and cried. She heard a click and the door slid open. She started to get up so she could escape when, Larry walked in.

"Oh thank God. Larry! Please get me out of here! Julia put me down here, and I don't know why. Help me please!"

"I'll help you get out of here, but you have to be very quiet so she doesn't hear us."

They went out to the car where she got in, and Larry offered her a bottle of water. She drank it quickly and started to feel fuzzy and then nothing. She was out cold.

Roofies are a wonderful thing, thought Larry. He'd been using them for years when he took his little trips away from home. Sarah should be out for a while, and it will give him plenty of time to get out of town and hide her away. Larry's phone rang, but he didn't answer it. He shut it off and returned it to his pocket because he wanted no interruptions while he was planning this trip. It was all different now that he already had a girl.

He pulled over at a rest area about half an hour later and tied Sarah up, put her in the back seat, and covered her and her bag up with a blanket so that if anyone saw her, they would think she was sleeping. He decided to get a little shut eye himself and kicked back in the front seat.

He got back on I-5 heading north about nine o'clock Saturday morning. He thought a change of scenery would be a great idea, and also, no one would know where to find them. Julia never asked where he was going when he left, and he never told her. He would leave, do his thing, and come back. He wasn't sure now if he could ever go back, or if he would have to leave Sarah where they ended up or kill her. He'd have to think about it. He continued to drive north on I-5 not sure where he would stop. He stopped for lunch and checked to see if Sarah was awake. She was still sleeping, so he grabbed some food and ate as he drove. He went up toward Washington but decided to stay closer to home. Dinnertime came, and he checked on Sarah. She was awake and screamed for him to let her go. He gagged her, covered her back up, and told her to be quiet, or she would die. She stopped moving, and he said, "Good girl. Now lay still while I check into this hotel. After that, I'll get us some food."

16

Luke was frantic when he called the police. He asked for Detective Hastings to see if he could come out to the house as he had new information. While he waited for the officer, he told his mother that she would tell the officer everything that she had done and nothing about what Luke had done. Detective Hastings showed up about half an hour later and sat with Luke and Julia and listened to her story. She never once mentioned that it was Luke's idea to take Sarah so that he could be her savior. She never once mentioned that he had left her in the fallout shelter and threatened to kill her. She took the blame for it all. It was the least she could do after what she did to him as a small boy.

"On your feet, ma'am. You're under arrest for the kidnapping of Sarah Wheeler. You have the right to remain silent. Anything you say will be used against you in a court of law. You have the right to have an attorney. If you cannot afford one, one will be appointed to you by the court. With these rights in mind, are you still willing to talk with me about the charges against you?"

"Yes," she said. "I'm so very sorry! I just wanted to scare her away from my son. He deserves so much better that that girl."

"You don't even know *that* girl!" Luke exclaimed. "How could you think that I would listen to you and who I should be dating? Tell the officer about Stella."

"Yes, of course. I met Stella and her mother and thought she would be perfect for Luke. I talked to her about him and told her that he might have a little crush on her, and she was thrilled. I didn't think she would take it as far as she did though—stalking, bullying, and trying to hurt Sarah. I really just wanted him to see that there were beautiful women out there that would throw themselves at him."

"Like you did to all those filthy men that used to come over and fuck you? Like I want to be with someone like you!" Julia flinched as if she'd been slapped. When had her son become so angry? *I did it to myself*, she thought.

Detective Hastings asked, "Julia, where is Sarah now?"

"I honestly have no idea. I put her downstairs Friday, and she isn't there today. Larry left town on Friday evening, and I can only hope he didn't find her down there and take her with him. He has some perverted sexual fantasies and leaves to take care of them once in a while."

"Where would he be headed?"

"He never goes to the same place as far as I know. He also uses drugs to get the girls to go home with him. He pretends he's saving them. He told me about this once, and I forbade him to ever speak about it again to me."

"What? Drugs? What kind of drugs? So help me, Mother, if he has drugged Sarah. I'll do something to you I may regret."

"Now, Luke, you don't know if he even has her. Just calm down until we find her. I'll need his license plate number and description of his car so I can put out an APB."

"Yes, of course."

She gave him the information he was looking for while Luke paced the living room and continued to glare at his mother. He didn't know what he would do if something happened to Sarah! Especially knowing about Larry and what a pervert he is. *Oh, Sarah. I'm so sorry for whatever happens to you! Please come home to me safe and please don't hate me because of this whole screwup.*

17

Larry pulled off of I-5 in Medford to check into a local hotel. He used an assumed name and paid cash. He was going to bring Sarah into the room, secure her, and then go get them some food. She hadn't made a peep after he told her to be quiet and given her more water. He guessed that the drugs in the water had helped to keep her quiet. When he went to go into his room, he pulled the blanket off her, and she looked like she was out cold. He sure hoped that he hadn't given her too many drugs. He'd hate for her to be in a coma. Although they didn't last long, just a couple of hours, it would screw up his plans for them. If she didn't wake up soon, he might just go out and find another girl and then they could all play together. If she didn't wake up at all, he could just dump her body. No one knew where she was or who she was with, so this might work to his advantage. She didn't move when he said, "Let's go, sleepy head." Lucky for him, it was dark out, and no one was paying attention to him, so he threw her over his shoulder fireman style and brought her into their room. He flopped her down on the bed and looked at how lovely she was. Although she was quiet and shy, she was a beauty.

He loosened the rope around her wrists so that he could tie her to the bed when her eyes flew open, and she fought him with all of her might. She kicked at him and punched him and screamed as loud as she could. "What the hell?" Larry was taken aback. He tried to ward off her punches and kicks, and when she started screaming he thought, *That's it. Someone's going to hear and call the police.* She landed a blow to his junk, and he folded like a well-worn piece of paper. Still screaming, Sarah jumped off the bed and ran to the door. She flung the door open and started to run.

She made it to the lobby crying and said, "You've got to help me. I've been kidnapped, and I just escaped! Please call the police." She begged. The clerk was speechless. "Hey! Call the police!" Sarah ran to the door and locked it and finished taking off the ropes.

Recovering, the clerk, Leo, asked while dialing 911, "What room were you in?"

"I have no idea! It was Larry Jackson."

"We don't have anyone by that name. Hang on. Yes, this is Leo from the Super 8, and I have a female here that says she's been kidnapped and just got away from the guy. She said his name is Larry Jackson, but we don't have anyone by that name. The last guy that checked in today was John Johnson. Ok. I'll go check it out." He hung up the phone and asked, "Is he still in that room?"

"I have no idea. I kicked him in the balls and ran out as fast as I could."

"I'm going to have to go look. You wait here for the cops."

"*No!* Don't leave me here alone. What if he comes up here and finds me? *Please!*"

"You can go back to my living quarters. He won't be able to get in. Lock the door behind me. I have a key." Leo left the office and walked over to the room that he had just rented. There was a man still lying on the floor in obvious pain.

"Hey, buddy! Do you need an ambulance? Why don't you get up from the floor and onto the bed?"

"I can't," Larry moaned. "It hurts too much to move!"

"Suit yourself." He left the room when he heard the squad car coming and went to flag them down so they could arrest the guy.

"Where is he?"

"He's in room 118. He was lying on the floor in quite a bit of pain. She said she kicked him in the balls."

"Show me where he is, and I'll take it from there" said the officer, impressed by the victim's bravery.

THE KIDNAPPING

"Right this way, Officer." Officer Plaino followed Leo to the room. Larry had moved but only to the edge of the bed. He saw the cop, and his face fell.

"On your feet!" Plaino said.

"Ok."

"You, sir, have a lot to explain. Who is that girl? Where did she come from? What did you think you were going to do with her?" asked the officer as he placed handcuffs on Larry's wrists.

"It was just an opportunity I couldn't pass up. She was in our fallout shelter, I was leaving town and thought I would bring her with me for entertainment. She is my son's girlfriend, and I have no idea how she got into that room. My wife and I are the only two that can get in there. My guess is that Julia put her in there, but I'm not sure why. Maybe she thinks the girl isn't good enough for our son. I thought I heard her mumbling about that one day."

Head hanging down, Larry left the hotel room and got in the squad car. In the meantime, Leo had gone back to the office, let himself in, and told Sarah that Larry was arrested.

"The police are going to want to talk to you, young lady. They need to know what happened and how in the world you got here."

"I know. I need to call my mom. Can I use your phone, please? I have no idea where my stuff is, and my cell is in my bag."

"Of course. I'm so sorry. I didn't think about that. She must be a wreck worried about you."

Sarah called their house number. No answer. She didn't leave a message. She wanted to talk to her mom and let her know that she was ok. She tried her mom's cell phone, and it was answered on the second ring.

When she heard her mother's voice, a chocked sob came out of Sarah, and she said, "Mom? Oh my God. Mom!" She burst into tears.

"Sarah? Sarah, is that you, baby?"

Swallowing down the tears, she said, "Yes, it's me."

A wail escaped from Lynda followed by a barrage of questions. "Oh my God. Where are you? Who are you with? Are you ok? What happened?"

Sarah laughed a little and said, "I'm ok. I'm with Larry. Julia put me in a secret room in their house, and he found me and brought me with him." She moved the phone away from her mouth and asked Leo, "Where am I?"

"Medford, Oregon," he replied.

"What? Oh, Mom, I'm in Medford, Oregon. He must have drugged me. I took a bottle of water from him and woke up in the car tied up in the back seat. He had told me he was going to bring me home, and I believed him. I didn't want him to know I was awake, so I pretended to still be sleeping. When he went to loosen the ropes on my wrists, I attacked him. I got away and Leo from the hotel called the police and Larry is under arrest. I still have to talk to the police and give my statement but can you come and get me?"

"Of course, sweetheart, of course. Just give me the name of the hotel."

"Super 8 in Medford and Mom please hurry. I want this all to be over with!"

"I'm on my way! Luke has been sick with worry. Do you want me to bring him with?"

"*No!* His family did this to me, and I don't ever want to see him again!"

"I understand, honey. You're going to have to talk to him eventually. You'll see him in school."

"I'll deal with it then but not now!"

Lynda called Detective Hastings to let him know that Sarah was alive and in Oregon and that she was on her way up there to get her.

"He took her across state lines? That can be considered a federal crime. He may go to jail for a long time."

"I sure hope so. I hope they throw the book at him!"

"I'm glad that she was able to get away. He didn't hurt her, did he?"

"Not from what she said, she hasn't been. Sarah told me that Julia kidnapped her and put her in a secret room in their house on

Friday. Larry went down there that same evening before he left and found her and took her with him and drugged her when they got in the car. That's all I know right now."

"Yes. We have Julia in custody right now. I just left their house about ten minutes ago and was going to stop by to tell you."

"Oh, thank God they caught her! You mean Luke turned in his own mother?"

"Yes. He's frantic about finding Sarah. Do you want me to call him and tell her she's all right?"

"No. Sarah said she didn't want to talk to him. I'm going to go get my daughter, and we'll hash it all out later."

18

Lynda drove the four-plus hours to Medford finding the hotel thanks to GPS. She pulled into the parking lot, jumped out of the car, and rushed to the lobby of the hotel.

"How can I help you, ma'am?" Leo asked when she entered the hotel.

"Where's my daughter? Where's Sarah?"

"Oh, you must be her mom. The police are questioning her in the back. They wanted to take her to the police station, but she insisted on staying here until you got here. Please follow me." Lynda followed Leo to the back of the hotel where she saw Sarah talking to an officer.

"Sarah!" she cried and ran to her daughter and enveloped her in a massive hug.

"*Mom*! Oh my God, I'm so happy to see you!" They both started to cry.

"You have no idea how worried I've been!" They hugged and cried.

Officer Plaino cleared his throat. "Hello, I'm Officer Plaino. Sarah has been recounting for me everything that has happened. This young lady has been through a lot in the last couple of days. I believe I am through questioning her, but if something comes up, I'll need a phone number to contact you."

"Hello, Officer Plaino. I'm Lynda. Yes, of course. You can call me anytime," she said and gave him her cell number. "Are we free to go?"

THE KIDNAPPING

"Yes, ma'am, you're free to go. Your daughter is a fighter, I'll give her that. She kept a cool head and fought her way out of what could have been a very dangerous situation. Take care now."

"Thank you so much. Are you ready, honey?"

"Yes, please. Let's get out of here!"

Lynda asked Sarah if she wanted to talk about it. "I'd really just like to get something to eat and get some rest. Can we stay in town for tonight and then go home tomorrow?"

"Of course. Oh, I should call your father and tell him that you are ok too. He's been worried sick since you didn't show up to the wedding."

"Oh no, that's right. I kinda forgot about it when Julia took me to her house after school. Can I use your cell? I have no idea where my bag is, and my cell was in it."

She proceeded to call her father. When he answered, he said, "Lynda, have you heard anything?"

"Daddy, it's me."

"What? Sarah? Is it really you?" She could hear him start to cry. "Oh, thank God my baby is alive! Are you hurt? Where are you?"

"I'm just a little tired, but I'm not hurt. I'm in Medford, Oregon. Mom is here and we are going to stay over tonight so I can get some rest."

"What happened?"

"I really don't want to talk about it right now. I need to get some rest. He drugged me, and I feel like I could sleep for a week." With that, she handed the phone to her mom.

"Who drugged you? What is happening?"

"Hi, Glenn. She really doesn't want to talk about it, and when she does, she'll tell us everything. I just want to get her home and safe. I'll let you know as soon as she's ready to talk about it."

They stayed at the Holiday Inn Express, ordered delivery, and got some much needed sleep before getting up early the next day to head home. Sarah was quiet in the car, almost too quiet. Lynda asked her if she was ok.

"Yeah, just thinking about everything. I don't know if I can ever look at Luke or talk to him again. I was starting to fall for him. I just don't see me getting past this to want to be with him ever again."

"You might not either, but I really don't think he had anything to do with it. Maybe after a few days at home, you'll change your mind and talk to him."

"Maybe, but right now, I don't want to even think about him! It hurts to think that his parents could do this to me, and what if he was in on it?"

"Try to rest, honey. Put it out of your mind for now. I know it's easier said than done, but you need to keep your strength up. There is going to be a lot going on once you get back home."

"That's what I'm afraid of!"

They arrived home on Tuesday afternoon. The drive seemed a lot longer than four hours. Sarah still didn't know where her bag and phone were. She told Lynda she was going up to her room to rest, and her mom said, "Good idea." Lynda called Detective Hastings to let him know they were back in town and that Sarah was resting. He asked if he could come by later to get her statement against Julia, and Lynda said that would be fine. While Sarah rested, Lynda thought she'd try to get some work done on the new listing she acquired and went to work in the living room.

A few hours later, Detective Hastings stopped by. Lynda went up to Sarah's room to find her quietly weeping. "Sarah, honey, what's wrong?"

"Everything! I can't find my stuff, the guy I was falling for has crazy parents, I've been kidnapped, and now I'm just supposed to go on like nothing happened? I don't think I can do this!"

"Oh, sweetheart, it will be ok, and no one expects you to go on like nothing has happened! You need time to process and heal. His parents may be crazy, but I don't think he is. Give it some time. I don't even expect you to go to school yet. I'll stop and pick up your homework until you are ready to go back. Does that sound ok for now?"

"I suppose so" she sniffled.

THE KIDNAPPING

"Detective Hastings is here and wants a statement from you if you're up to it."

"I guess there's no time like the present."

They went downstairs to talk to him. Sarah told him everything that she could remember stating that there were chunks of her memory that she still didn't have.

Hastings said, "He admitted to giving you roofies to keep you quiet that's why you don't remember everything."

"He *drugged* my daughter with a date-rape drug? That son of a bitch! It's a good thing he's in jail. He might have ended up in the morgue if I had found him."

"I know this is upsetting news, Lynda. I'm sorry to have to tell you about it, but now Sarah at least knows why she doesn't recall the whole ordeal, and maybe right now, it's best that she doesn't. Sarah, did he touch you in any way that you can remember?"

"Not that I can remember. Any time that I was awake though, I was clothed, and we were driving. It seemed like we drove for a very long time and still only ended up in Medford. Why is that, did he say?"

"He just said that he was going to take you to Washington but didn't like how close it was to the border, so he came back down this way. It's a good thing he did too. If he would have gone into Canada, he'd get put in jail there and then he'd have to be extradited back to California. He's in jail in Oregon right now. I've talked to the police there, and we'll have him down here in no time and charge him with several crimes. Sarah, would you like to tell me anything else?"

"I think that covers what I can remember. The police in Oregon have my statement, too, if there are other questions. I'm just so happy to be home!" Suddenly there was a knock at the door, and it was shoved open.

"*Sarah!*" It was Luke, and he was running in to see her.

"Luke! Get out, now!" Sarah yelled at him. He stopped in his tracks.

"Sarah! I'm so happy that you're ok!" He started to walk toward her again.

Lynda stood up and said, "*Stop,* Luke! She asked you to leave and I think you better. Don't make this any harder on her than it already is."

He stopped but didn't leave and said, "I'm sorry, Sarah, for everything that has happened to you! I love you and would never do anything to hurt you! I'll go for now but won't stop coming around until you talk to me."

"That might not ever happen," she said and turned away from him so she didn't have to look at him. Luke turned and went out the door.

"How did he know I was back?"

Detective Hastings said, "I told him. I didn't think it would hurt for him to know you were ok. I'm sorry. I shouldn't have done that."

"No, you shouldn't have!"

"Again, I apologize. I'll be going. I have everything I need for now."

"Thank you, Detective," Lynda said.

19

The Oregon police called Lynda to tell her they had located Sarah's bag in Larry's car and that an officer would bring it down to them. She went up to Sarah's room to tell her the good news, but she was sleeping. She left quietly and decided to call Luke and get some more information on what he knew about this whole ordeal. He answered right away and asked if he could come over to talk to her face to face. She said sure since Sarah was sleeping, she didn't think it was a bad idea. When he arrived, they went to the living room and discussed what had happened. He told her what he knew about Julia's roll in the kidnapping, and she told him what she knew. He was so angry, his face turning redder by the minute.

He said, "I'd like to strangle that man!"

"He's your father, Luke, but I can understand how you feel. I feel the same."

"No, he's not my father! He's some guy my mom married because he had money. She was a whore when I was a kid and did things that she should be in jail for. I don't really want to talk about it though, it will just make me angrier."

"Maybe if you talk about it, you can start to heal. It seems like you are very angry when you talk about your parents. I'm a good listener and would like to know what makes you so mad. If you and Sarah are to have any kind of future together, she's going to want to know the good and the bad about you."

"I really don't want to, but if you think it would help to talk to you, maybe I should. I don't want there to be any secrets between Sarah and me, and I trust you, unlike my own parents."

He told her everything. What his mom did to him as a child, finding out what a pervert Larry was, and hoping to God that he didn't have Sarah, locking his own mother in the fallout shelter, all of it. Lynda sat there amazed at this young man and what he had been through. She felt hot tears running down her face.

"Oh, Luke, I'm so sorry for all that has happened to you. You put on a very brave face! But why now? Why did you decide to do something about it now and not years ago?"

"After we moved here, I saw Sarah and just knew that she was the one for me. She's perfect, beautiful, smart, everything I want in a woman. I know we're young, but I've never felt this way about anyone before. I don't even think I knew what real love was until I met her. I surely didn't feel love as a kid and just the way she looks at me turns me all inside out. Do you know what I'm saying?"

Smiling, Lynda said, "Oh Luke, I do, and it makes this mother very happy to hear you say all of those wonderful things about my daughter. I know she cares for you, but she may not want to talk to you for a while because she feared you may have had something to do with it." He looked hurt and then angry all over again.

"If they have taken away the one thing that I finally love, I'll never forgive them!"

Sarah was sitting on the stairs listening to this conversation, crying, smiling, and crying all over again. He really did love her! She knew she loved him, too, but was still afraid to tell him after all of this. Was love strong enough to get them through this? She wasn't sure but decided to find out. She went down the stairs into the living room and cleared her throat. They both looked up to see her standing there with tears on her face.

"Mom, can Luke and I be alone please?"

"Of course." Lynda went upstairs to give them some privacy. Sarah stood in the middle of the living room, not wanting to get to close to him.

"Sarah, why are you crying?"

"I was listening to what you were telling my mom. Please don't interrupt me until I'm done with what I have to tell you."

"Ok."

"First, I think I love you too. I don't know if it will be enough to get us through this or not, but I wanted you to know. Second, I think you need to tell the police what you did to your mother. It is essentially what she did to me, and it was terrifying. Maybe they'll go easy on you since you are still a minor. Third, I want them to both be in jail for a very long time, and I hope that you and I can work together to make that happen. I don't want there to be secrets between us either and I have to know, did you know anything that your mom had planned?"

"*No*! God, Sarah, how can you even ask that? I knew I was in love with you the minute we had our first conversation. I would never do anything to hurt you! I wanted to hurt my mom for what she did to me, so I gave her a taste of her own medicine. She didn't like it, and you're right, I need to confess to what I did. She bought me so many expensive things to try to make up for it, but she damaged me; and I hope with time, therapy, and you, I can become a better person. I will work with you every step of the way to make sure that they pay for what they did! Will you help me, Sarah? Help me deal with this anger and sadness? Help me to heal and become a better person for myself and for us?"

"It sounds like a lot, but I would really like to try." She moved toward him, and he stood up with open arms. She fell against him and continued to cry. He stroked her hair and murmured that he loved her and that they could get through anything together. She finally stopped, dried her eyes, and said, "What do we do now?"

"I'm not sure. Are you hungry?" They laughed, called Lynda downstairs, and made something to eat.

"Have you two patched things up?"

"We're going to try to get on with our lives together," Sarah stated.

"Yes, together," Luke confirmed.

20

Since Luke's parents were both in jail, he had to find somewhere else to live. Lynda said that he could stay with them in the spare room until other arrangements could be made. He would be eighteen in two months and then could live in the house by himself. He was excited about staying with them. He felt such love and warmth there. "I'll go home and pack some things," he said. Just as he was getting ready to leave, there was a knock at the door. It was the cop from Medford with Sarah's bag. They thanked him for bringing it down, and Sarah checked in it for her cell. Thank God it was there! She checked it and saw that there were a number of texts and voice mails. She looked through the texts and listened to the messages, most of them from Luke and her mom.

The last message she heard was from Stella threatening her yet again. She saved that and would give that to the police. Why won't she stop? Enough is enough.

"Mom, is Stella in jail for everything that she's done to me?"

"I thought so. Why?"

"She left me another threatening message. I'm going to have to give it to the police."

"Maybe because she's young, she's on house arrest. I'll find out from Officer Hastings." She called him to find out about Stella. He said that she was in jail and was allowed to use the phone once a day.

Lynda said, "Maybe someone should monitor who she calls. She called and threatened my daughter yet again."

"You're kidding me!"

THE KIDNAPPING

"No, I'm not, and I'm extremely irritated by this. Sarah is going to give you the message. Would you like to hear it now?"

"I'll swing by in a little bit, and I can hear it then."

"Ok, thank you," she said hanging up. "Hastings is coming over to listen to that message, honey."

"Ok. I just want things to go back to normal. Is that too much to ask?"

"No, honey, it's not. Hopefully soon, they will be!"

"Now when Luke comes back, I want to sit down with you guys and make some house rules." She put her hand up when Sarah was going to protest. "Just a minute. You two are in love, and things happen."

"Aw, Mom, that's not cool! I don't want to talk about this in front of Luke!"

"Why? Haven't you two discussed the possibility of being intimate?"

"Well, no. We've barely kissed. We've been studying, and I've been learning to drive. He's had football practice and then his mom kidnapped me. There really hasn't been time or much thought about it on my part at least. It's kind of embarrassing!"

"It's a perfectly natural thing that happens between a man and a woman. I just want you to be safe, that's all. If you don't want me to bring it up, you'll have to promise me that you will be responsible and talk to him yourself."

"Fine. I'll talk to him, but it won't be as soon as he comes back."

"Sarah, are you sure you're ok with everything that happened? Larry didn't hurt you in any way did he?" her mom asked hoping that he hadn't touched her, and she was too afraid to say anything. "No, he didn't, and after hearing Luke talk about everything, I think I'm doing ok. I'm really just anxious for this to all be over with."

"I know. So am I. I'm sure there will be more than one trial that we are going to be involved in as well. I'm not sure if they will put Julia and Larry on trial at the same time, or if those will be separate and then there will be one for Stella. I think that we really should put out a restraining order on her since she continues to call. Every time she calls, it will be another strike against her, and she will just be hurting herself by continuing to harass you."

"Ugh! I just want to be done with all of it. I wish I could go to sleep for about a week, and it would all be over."

Her mother smiled at her sadly and said, "Unfortunately, that's not going to happen, but we will do this together. Whatever it takes to make you safe again, I'm going to do it!"

"I know I don't say this enough, Mom, but thank you for everything that you do for me! I love you so much!" Sarah got off the couch, went over to her mom and gave her a big bear hug. She then ran up to her room, leaving her mother smiling after her.

Several weeks after Sarah's return and Luke moving into the house, Lynda decided to focus more time and energy into selling that house in Chico. Normally, houses this expensive took a while to sell, but she was determined to sell it sooner rather than later. She did a local radio spot, a TV commercial, and hoped for more interest this time around. She was working from home when she got a call about setting up a showing, and they wanted to do it right away, so she set it up for five that evening. *Wow, that was fast*, she thought. She finished up what she was doing, went up and showered, changed and texted Sarah that she would be showing the Chico house at five o'clock, so she and Luke were on their own for dinner. She locked up, left the house, and went to the office to grab some stuff she needed for the showing. She always made sure she had the paperwork with in case someone wanted to make an offer on the place while they were there.

21

The house in Chico was empty, so she went over to check it out and make sure that it was presentable. When she pulled up to the house, there was a car in the driveway. She knew better than to assume it's the party she's going to meet and watched to see if there was anyone in the car. It was 4:30 p.m., and if it was the people that wanted to see it, they should be in their car. She didn't see anyone in the car. Maybe they are looking around back or something. She drove by, turned around down the street, and came back, driving slowly, hoping to see someone. She didn't, so she called the person that she was supposed to be showing the house to.

"Hello, is this Mr. Willis? Oh, hi, this is Lynda, the realtor. Are you at the house already?"

"Oh hi, Lynda. No, I'm not at the house yet. Why?"

"There is a car in the driveway, but no one is in the car, and I was just checking to see if it was you. I'm a little cautious about getting out of my car alone when I don't see someone. I'll be at the house waiting for you, but I'll be in my car."

"I should be there in about ten minutes. I understand about you not getting out of your car. I wouldn't want anything to happen to you. See you soon."

"Ok, Mr. Willis. I'll see you soon."

Lynda sat in her car on the street watching the house. No movement outside, and nothing seemed to be going on inside, so she waited for Mr. Willis. He showed up about ten minutes later, pulled up behind her, and got out of his car. She exited hers as well.

They introduced themselves, and Mr. Willis insisted that she call him Charles.

"Well, Charles, shall we go in?"

"I'm really curious about this car. Have you seen anything at all? No one outside?"

"Nothing has moved since I've been sitting here. I don't know whose car that is, and frankly, I'm concerned. I could call the police to alert them of the vehicle, or we could go look inside. I'm not sure if someone has broken in and is living in there, or if someone just parked the car here and is visiting someone in the neighborhood."

"I'd feel better if we knew whose car that was, so maybe we should call the police just to be on the safe side?"

"That's fine with me. I'll call them right now." She called the nonemergency police in Chico to let them know there was a strange vehicle in front of the house that she was selling and wanted someone to come out and check it out. She told them that her and a client were there to look at the house but were concerned about going in. The operator told her that they had a car in the neighborhood and that someone would be there shortly. Lynda thought to herself, *I really need to stop having so much interaction with the police.*

Charles and Lynda sat in her car chatting while they waited for the police. Charles told Lynda he was recently divorced and that he was a prosecuting attorney new to the area from St. Paul, Minnesota.

"What brings you to Chico? It's so much smaller than St. Paul."

"Exactly! And warmer, and it's far away from my ex-wife."

Lynda smiled and said, "I have an ex-husband who just got remarried, and I must say, I'm glad we don't live in the same town."

"How long have you been divorced?"

"About a year and a half. We have a fifteen-soon-to-be-sixteen-year-old daughter who has been going through some troubling times lately, and it would be so much easier if her father was more involved. I'm doing the best that I can, though, and we are happy. Oh, the police are here." They got out of her car, met the officer, and he told them to stay by the car while he went to check things out.

THE KIDNAPPING

Lynda told him that she could open the coded lock on the door if he wanted her to, and he said, "Not yet. I want to check around the back and see if there is anyone back there first."

"Ok, let me know if we can help at all."

"You two just sit tight, and I'll let you know." They stood outside of the car, waiting for the policeman to come back from the backyard. It seemed like a very long time, and he finally came back and said, "That is one big backyard! Ok. Give me the code for the lock. I'm going to go inside. You guys hang on until I get back." Lynda gave him the code, and he went in the front door.

Officer Layton caught the call to check out a mysterious vehicle in a driveway of a vacant house that was for sale. *Really?* he thought, *this is what I get called out for?* He was happy to be doing something instead of just driving around looking for trouble to happen. He headed out to the neighborhood and thought, *Wow. This is a nice neighborhood. I would never be able to afford anything around here!* He pulled up behind the two vehicles on the street in front of the house. *Ah, that must be the folks that called.* He got out of his car as did they, introduced himself, and asked if they had seen anything at all. Neither of them had, so he said he was going to go check out the back and be back up. He walked up to the car and peered inside. Strange, there were keys hanging from the ignition. He tried the door, and it was unlocked. He opened it and looked around inside but found nothing else that concerned him. He went through to the backyard to see if he could find the owner of the car. The yard was massive! It was fenced in all the way around and there were several out buildings to check. He walked to the first one, opened it, and found nothing but lawn tools. Next stop was what looked like an oversized doll house. It, too, was empty. The farthest building was big enough for a car, and it was padlocked. He walked along the fence all the way to the back, followed it around the back, and then up to the house. There was nothing back here.

He walked back out to the front of the house where he asked Lynda for the code to get in. He went to the door, put in the code, and opened the door. When the door opened, he was hit with an overwhelming smell! His hand flew to his face to cover his nose. What was that? It smelled like rotting fish or something. He looked around on the first floor, nothing. He hadn't located the smell either. Second floor, nothing. The basement was last. He took out his flashlight and headed down the stairs. He thought he heard a soft thump, so he drew his weapon. The smell was getting worse down here, and he flipped lights on as he went. When he got to the bottom of the stairs, he stopped dead in his tracks. There was a man sitting on the floor in the middle of family room, and it appeared he was the cause of the smell. There was a buzzing of sorts coming off the man, and as the officer walked around him, he saw why. There were flies in all various stages of life on this man. He no longer had eyeballs, things were crawling out of his mouth, and Officer Layton gagged. He rushed back up the stairs calling for backup and CSI. He ran out the front door just in time to stop himself from throwing up. He knew he would contaminate the scene if he didn't get out of that house. Lynda and Charles saw the officer fly out the front door. What in the world could be in there? He looked white as a sheet.

"Officer? Officer Layton, what is it?"

"There is a dead man in the basement, and it looks like he's been there for a while. I've called for backup and CSI. You won't be showing this house any time soon."

"What? Oh my God! Who is it? How did he get in there?" Lynda asked.

"I have no idea who it is. I didn't check him for ID. It doesn't appear that there was forced entry, at least not the front door, but there could be from somewhere else. I was just looking for someone to be there that might belong to the car, not how they might have gotten in. Excuse me, I have to call in a description of the car and see if I can find out who it's registered to. You folks will have to answer some questions when the detectives get here, so please bear with us for a little bit." The officer called dispatch to give them the VIN and description of the car. They gave him a name that the car was registered in, but it was a woman's name, so he wondered if the car was stolen. He asked Lynda if he knew a Marilyn Stuart. She said, "Why, no, that name doesn't sound familiar to me at all."

THE KIDNAPPING

The detectives showed up about twenty minutes later. They approached Charles and Lynda and asked who had called it in. Lynda said that she did as she was the realtor that was selling the property. "We'd like to ask you a few questions, if that's all right."

"That will be fine," she replied. "What time did you notice the car here?"

"I got here about four thirty and the car was here when I got here. I drove by and called Charles to see if it was him since he wanted a showing, but it wasn't."

"When was the last time you showed the house?"

"It has been several weeks since I've shown it. The last people I showed it to were a doctor, his wife, and three kids. I've only shown it to three couples so far."

"Ok. Hang on for a little bit longer, please? We're going to go in the house and look around."

"Ok. Thank you, Detective."

Charles looked at Lynda and said, "Well, this is quite unfortunate! I was really looking forward to seeing this house. I think it would be perfect for me."

"Isn't it a little bit big for a single man?"

"Not really. I like a big house. I've got two older children, and they are both getting married soon. I am hoping for grandchildren, and with a larger house, I can configure the rooms any way that *I* want to. If I want to have a home gym, I can have one, and no one can tell me it's not practical."

"Well, this house is definitely big enough for children, grandchildren, and parties; that's for sure. I'm sorry that you won't be able to look at it today. I will probably never be able to sell it now! I'll have to call the owners and let them know what's happened. I sure hope the detectives hurry up. I'd like to get home to my daughter. She's had a rough patch lately, and I don't like her to be home alone for too long."

"Didn't you say that she was almost sixteen? Surely she's old enough to be home alone."

"After what she's been through, I don't even think she *wants* to be."

"Maybe you could tell me about it over coffee one day?"

"I don't like to talk about it much. It was a very scary time and still very fresh in my mind."

"I am a lawyer, so it would be in the strictest of confidence if you told me anything about it."

"Well, maybe. Oh, here come the detectives."

"Thank you both for waiting. The guy in the house is named David Smalley. Do you know him?" one of them asked Lynda.

"No. That isn't the name of anyone I showed this house to. I wonder how he got in."

"We're still trying to determine that. Unless someone put him in there that knew it was vacant and for sale. We won't know until we do a more thorough search of the entire property. I'll take your cell phone numbers in case we have more questions, but there is no point in your hanging around here." They gave the detectives their cell numbers and walked back toward their cars.

"Lynda, I would really like to take you out for that coffee and get to know you better. I might even be able to give you some advice for your daughter. Free, of course."

"Well, Charles, I think I would like that. Call me in a few days, and hopefully, this mess will be straightened out."

"I'd also like to hire you to find me a home similar to this one, if you could, please. I'd like a big house and around this area would be great. If you find something like it, call me, and we can get together to look at it."

"Ok, Charles. I'll start on it right away. Thank you." Lynda smiled at him. This day was shaping up to be ok. *I wonder who the man in the house is.* She put it out of her mind and went back home.

22

When she got home, all the lights in the house were on, and the door was wide open again. *What is with this kid and leaving the door open?* She went in, and the house was trashed! Books thrown around, more pictures broken, curtains ripped, and sofa cushions cut up. *What the hell?* She yelled, "Sarah! Luke!" No answer. *Oh my God. Not again.* She grabbed her cell and called 911.

The operator answered, and she cried, "My house has been broken into and trashed. I can't find my daughter and her boyfriend. Please hurry!"

"I'll send someone right over. Please stay on the line with me. Are you still in the house?"

"Yes. I'm looking for my daughter and her boyfriend. There's no answer when I call for them."

"I would suggest you exit the house and wait for the officers to come to you."

"I need to find my daughter! I don't want to wait outside." She could hear sirens by then and told the operator that as she walked out of the house to meet the police.

"Thank you, ma'am, and I hope you find them."

"So do I!"

The police arrived not even a minute later. She told them the house had been vandalized and that she couldn't find her daughter and her boyfriend. They told her to stay put and that they'd check out the house. She stood by her car and tried Sarah's cell, it went right to voice mail. She tried Luke's cell. It did the same thing. She became a little frantic, wracking her brain to see if the kids had said they were doing anything that night. She tried her ex-husband to see if maybe they made a trip out to see him. No dice. When she told Glenn that Sarah and Luke were both missing and that each of their phones went to voice mail, he was dumbfounded. Twice in a matter of months? How can this be happening!

The officers came out of the house, and they were alone. "Sorry, ma'am. There's no one in the house. We didn't find a burglar, your daughter, or her boyfriend. It's safe for you to go back in, and we'll come in and take a statement from you." She went into the house just sickened at what had been done. This day just went from not bad to terrible! She texted her daughter and Luke and got no response.

She called Detective Hastings's cell, which he answered and said, "Lynda, is everything ok?"

"Oh, I just don't know! Someone broke into the house, trashed it, and Sarah and Luke are both missing!"

"What? I'll be right there."

"Please hurry. I don't know what to do!" she sobbed into the phone.

"Hang on, I'm coming."

He arrived in record time, and when he saw Lynda, gave her a hug and asked her to tell him everything. She started with the showing at the house and what had happened there and then coming home to find this. She was exhausted after telling the whole story, and Hastings was speechless.

"I'll follow up with the Chico police about the man in the house, but we have to figure out where Sarah and Luke are. This is maddening! Who has it in for these two or you for that matter?"

"I don't know! I can't lose her! She's my world, and she's already been through enough this year."

The officers came to get her statement, and Detective Hastings told them that he had gotten it from her already. "We need to go over to Luke's house and see if they are there. C'mon, Lynda, you're riding with me. Let CSI take care of this. You guys should come with us as well, just in case."

THE KIDNAPPING

The police went over to Luke's house with sirens blaring and lights flashing. Lynda was in the squad with Detective Hastings biting at her nails. She was so afraid of what they might find there, she didn't even want to think about it. She tried both of their cells again and nothing. When they got to the house, Hastings told her to stay in the car unless he said that she could get out. She reluctantly agreed to wait. He banged on the door, hoping that one of them would answer it. No answer. Shit! He tried the doorknob, it was locked. He took a step back and kicked at the door. It didn't open the first time. He tried again, bingo, the doorframe splintered, and the door swung in. He and the other officers entered the home and searched it from top to bottom. There was no one there. He remembered the bomb shelter and wondered if they could be in there. He radioed dispatch to see if they could find someone that would be able to get into the shelter. They told him that they would send someone over right away. When he came out, Lynda could tell by the expression on his face that he didn't find anyone there. He came over to the car and told her that someone was coming to try to open the bomb shelter to see if they were in there. Her heart sank. Where could they be? How could this be happening all over again?

23

She was absolutely elated that she had found them together. Now she could take out all of her frustrations on both of them while the other one watched! No one would suspect her! It was perfect! Sarah and Luke were tied up, blindfolded, and shoved onto the floor of the van. She didn't want anyone to see them. She needed to get them out of town before anyone knew they were missing. In the distance, she heard sirens. *I sure hope those aren't for me!* She couldn't worry about that now. She had to get them someplace that she could show them both how much she truly hated them. Having to sit in jail because that little *bitch* wouldn't leave Luke alone. *His mother told me he had a crush on me, but he wouldn't even give me the time of day. That old hag had lied to me!* She didn't think that Sarah was good enough for her son, and Stella had agreed! When she found out that he was living with her and her mother, that was the last straw! She was going to hurt them both as badly as she had been hurt. She wanted them to suffer like she did all those months in jail! *Unstable? I'll show you who's unstable! You haven't seen anything yet!*

While she drove, she played different scenarios in her head and finally came up with a good one. Once she could find a place to stop, she'd show them a thing or two. At the next rest area, she pulled over to check on the two lovebirds. When she got out and opened up the van, she was shoved to the ground and someone heavy landed on her and she lost her breath. She was gasping for air and saw that it was Luke. She tried to fight him off, but he was too heavy. She laid there trying to catch her breath and insisted he get off her.

THE KIDNAPPING

"Not on your life!" he growled at her. "How could you do this? How could you put us through this kind of thing again? What is wrong with you? Don't tell me all that shit about you being in love with me, it's bullshit! My mother told me that she sicced you on Sarah, and it has gotten way out of control. You listen to me and listen good. I don't like you. I can't even stand to be this close to you! You make me sick!" He shouted the words in her face.

She laughed in his and said, "*You* make *me* sick! Playing house with that little goody-goody like you were married or something. You two deserve each other. You're both damaged goods! Get off me, you fuck!"

"I won't until the police arrive, or maybe I should just kill you and then this would all be over once and for all."

Sarah came up from behind him and said, "No, Luke, she needs to go back to jail where she belongs. Maybe even to a mental ward. Hey, maybe she can share a jail cell with your mom."

Sarah found Stella's cell and called 911. She then called her mom and told her what Stella had done. Lynda nearly passed out from relief. Why in the world does all this bad shit keep happening?

Lynda hung up the phone with Sarah and told Detective Hastings what had happened. "I heard she had been released but thought she had been sent for a psych evaluation and that she wouldn't be around here for a while. Now she'll go to jail for a lot longer than she did before. How did Sarah sound? I'm going to assume it was Stella who trashed the house as well?"

"She didn't say. We'll just have to wait until they get home."

Sarah and Luke put Stella in the van and, when the police came, gave their statements, and they were told they could leave.

"Only problem, Officer. The van is hers, and we have no way to get back home."

"Oh yes, we'll send you home in one of the squads."

"That would be fantastic! I can't wait to get back home!" Sarah exclaimed.

She sure was tired of people trying to hurt her! For a small town, Paradise sure didn't seem like it lately! A long hot shower and a long night of sleep is what she was wishing for. She and Luke climbed in the back of the squad car, and it was about an hour before they got home. They talked quietly about what had just happened and held hands to give each other strength. When they pulled up in the squad car, the officer walked with them to the door. Sarah was opening the door at the same time her mom was, and they both gasped. Seeing it was her mom, Sarah smiled and gave her a big hug.

"Sarah! Luke! Are you guys all right? What did she do to you? How did she get you out of the house? Who trashed everything?"

"Let's all go sit down, and they can tell us all about it, Lynda," said Detective Hastings.

"Yes, ok. Let's go sit down, and you can tell us everything. We'll need to call your father, too, Sarah. He's worried sick."

The kids took turns telling what happened. It seemed that Stella had gotten out of jail and gone right over to Sarah's as soon as she could get away from her mother. She had stolen a gun from her father's gun safe and came in gun first ordering Sarah to tie up Luke. Once that was done, she grabbed Sarah by the hair and tied her up to a chair on the opposite side of the living room from Luke. She then went throughout the house and trashed it. Pictures, awards, knickknacks, anything that had been in Sarah's room, or anything that had a picture of Sarah, she destroyed. All of her new clothes had been shredded. She broke the mirror in Sarah's bedroom, sliced open her mattress, and went completely crazy destroying everything she could get her hands on. She then came back downstairs and took them both out to the van where she put them on the floor. She hadn't checked the knots on Luke for security. Sarah hadn't tied them tight, but they were tight enough, so he had to work on getting out of them. He finally did in the van, and when Stella stopped and opened the van, he pounced.

They were done retelling their story to which Detective Hastings said, "My goodness, she is really evil! I hope she gets put somewhere that can help her and that she can never get out of again."

"*Agreed!*" all three of them said at the same time and then smiled.

It was Lynda's turn to tell them the story of what happened to her that day. Once she finished, she said, "I don't know about any of you, but I'm exhausted. This has been a very trying day, and I need to rest. The only bonus in the deal is that I got a new client out of it and maybe a date."

"What? Really, Mom? You're going to go on a date?"

"I might. I haven't decided. He seems to be really nice, and he wants me to find him a house to buy."

"Awesome! That's great, Mom!"

"That really is great, Lynda!" said Luke. "You're a heck of a lady and a good catch in my opinion."

Blushing, she said, "Oh, go on, you guys. I don't even know if I'm going to go."

"I can check him out of you, if you'd like, Lynda," the detective offered.

"Oh no, I don't think that's necessary."

"Well, pardon me for saying so but with everything that's happened to your family lately, don't you think that you should be a little more cautious? It doesn't take much to run a background check on him, and I can let you know if he comes up shady at all. Or you could just forget about him and go out with me?" he asked sheepishly.

She looked at him and the kids looked at him and they excused themselves. Although Sarah wanted to stay to see what would happen, she thought this was a rather private moment. She also knew that she needed to make a bed on the floor since her mattress was trashed and decided now was as good of a time as any.

"Why, Detective Hastings, are you asking me out to protect me or because you like me?"

"Please call me Brad. I like you, *and* I want to protect you. What do you say? I can make dinner for us."

"You cook?"

"I do a lot of things outside of my job. I'm not always on duty."

"You always seem to be on duty when I call."

"It's because it's *you* that I come over every time you call." He walked over to her, looked deeply into her eyes, and said, "What do you think? Dinner at my place tomorrow night, just the two of us?" He was standing so close it was hard to catch her breath.

"That sounds great. What can I bring?"

"Just you and your lovely smile. Be there about seven o'clock." He leaned down quickly and planted a kiss on her lips and turned around and left. Her emotions all over the place, she decided to go upstairs take a shower and deal with everything else tomorrow.

24

After a good night's sleep, things looked better in the morning. Well, almost everything. The house was still a mess, and she wanted to find out about the man at the house she was supposed to be selling. She called the insurance company to report the property damage to her house and was told someone would be out there today to write up an estimate. She hung up with them and then called the Chico police station to see if she could find out anything about the case. She was told that there was nothing they could tell her because she wasn't the owner of the home. She asked the police if the owners had been contacted, and they said yes. She decided to call them as soon as she hung up with the police to see if they still wanted to leave it for sale. When she called the owners of the home, they were so upset they didn't know what to do. They asked her if she had any advice, and she said she thought they should take it off the market for now until everything calmed down. They decided to take her advice, so Lynda told them she would take care of everything on her end to remove the listing. *This is a real bummer for me*, thought Lynda. *I was really counting on selling that house.* She did get a new client out of the deal, and he wanted a house like that one, so maybe it would be ok in the long run. Speaking of her new client, she should get to work on finding him a house. She decided to work from home until the insurance adjuster showed up so she could get her estimate.

    Sarah came down a little later and saw what Stella had really done to the house. Her room aside, the rest of the house was a complete mess. Sarah asked her mom if they should start cleaning it up, and she said, "No. The insurance adjuster is coming over, and we shouldn't touch anything, so they get the full effect of what happened here."

Sarah ate breakfast and asked, "Where's Luke?"

"He was up right away this morning and left. I'm not sure where he went."

"Oh. I'll text him to see if he went to school or what."

"Good idea. I'm going to work from home until I see the adjuster. You're not going to school today, are you?"

"If it's ok with you, I'd really like to stay home and get some things cleaned up. I know, I'll wait until after the adjuster has been here to clean my room. I can't believe that she did this! She shredded all of my clothes, my mattress, my whole room is trashed. Can we go shopping again? I don't have anything to wear except some really old stuff that might not even fit any more."

"We'll have to go some time tonight. I really want to get something ready for Mr. Willis and set up some showings for him. I also want to know what the adjuster thinks. We're going to have to get an entire bedroom for you, a new couch, clothes, the list is a mile long."

"Ok. I'm going up to my room and see what is left for me to wear then I'm going to take a long hot shower." She went upstairs, checked her clothes, and found some things that she could wear that weren't too bad and went in to take that long hot shower.

Once she was finished cleaning up and getting ready for her day, she checked her phone and found nothing back from Luke. She decided to call her dad and let him know that she was ok and what had happened. After she got off the phone with him, she called Luke's cell to see if he would answer. No answer. She was growing concerned now especially after everything that has happened. She texted him again and told him to reply ASAP because she was worried. She went back downstairs where her mom was talking to a woman about the damage in the house. *Must be the adjuster*, she thought. The woman walked around taking notes and pictures as she went through the house. Lynda said to Sarah, "Why don't you take her up to your room and show her everything up there?" Sarah brought the adjuster to her room, and she did the same thing—more photos, notes, and questions. Once they were finished, they went back downstairs.

Lynda asked the adjuster, "How long do you think it will be before I will get a check so that I can replace some of these items?"

"Well, I will see if I can issue you at least enough to get a mattress and some clothes for Sarah, but normally, these things take a couple of weeks."

"A couple of weeks? How are we supposed to move on with our lives if we have to wait for weeks to replace these things?"

"I'll get a hold of my boss, and I'll bet the she will let me cut you a check later on today. I'll call you as soon as I talk to her about this unique situation."

"A check today would be very helpful! We were going to go shopping and get some things today, and if we have the check, that will make it easier on the pocketbook. We had just gone and gotten Sarah a whole new wardrobe a couple of weeks ago."

"I totally understand, and I will call you as soon as I talk to her."

"Wonderful. Thank you so much! Have a great day!" she said closing the door behind the adjuster.

"Well, that would be helpful to get that money today. Any word from Luke?"

"No, and I'm starting to get very worried about him. He always answers his texts."

"Maybe he's in school?"

"I don't think so. I don't know what to do besides wait to hear back from him. What if that nutjob Stella had another plan for Luke? What if she hired someone else to kidnap him if she failed?"

"Do you really think so? Maybe you're just being paranoid."

"Maybe, but we don't know where he is, he isn't texting me back, he didn't answer his phone, and I don't know what else to think. Mom, what if she really did something crazy like that?"

"We'll just have to give it some time. I don't think we can report him missing since he's only been gone a couple of hours."

"Can you call Detective Hastings? Can you just ask him if there is anything we can do?"

"Ok. I'll call him and ask." Lynda called the detective, and he said that he would drive by Luke's house to see if the teen was there. "He said he'd drive by his house to see if he is there, but that's all that we can do right now, honey. I'm sorry."

"Ok. I'll just have to wait." Sarah continued to worry about Luke and where he could have gone, why he didn't tell anyone, and why he wasn't getting back to her.

25

When Luke left that morning, he had every intention of getting to the bottom of this Stella thing with his mother. He went to the prison where she was being held and asked to see her. He was told that he could see her for only fifteen minutes. When his mother came to the visitors lounge, she had on an orange jumpsuit and looked thin and sickly. Her face lit up like a Christmas tree when she saw her son. Beaming, she went to the table.

"Oh, Luke, I knew you wouldn't forget about me in here! How are you?"

"Mother, I didn't come here to make small talk. I came here to tell you to get Stella off our backs! She is seriously deranged, and now she's in jail for kidnapping as well. Didn't you tell her before to leave us alone? This has got to stop. I'm staying with Lynda and Sarah now, and everything is perfect! Stop trying to mess up my life!"

"Luke, I did what you asked. I tried to scare Sarah a little bit by putting her in the fallout shelter. Why are you being like this to me?"

"Because now I have what I want. I don't need you any longer, and that psycho needs to leave us alone!"

"But, Luke!"

"No buts! Either you tell her to leave us alone, or she will not be around to speak to ever again. Are we clear?"

"Luke, I—"

"*I said are we clear?*" he shouted at her.

"Yes, perfectly. I just don't know how I'm going to get a message to her if she's in jail."

"That's not my problem, it's yours. She might even be here. I don't know. Goodbye, Mother."

With that, he got up and left her with her mouth hanging open and wondering if she would ever get the love of her son back. *Probably not,* she thought, *I've been a horrible, rotten, conniving mother. I don't blame him if he never speaks to me again.* She was led back to her cell.

Luke looked at his phone after his visit with his mother and had several texts and a voice mail from Sarah. He didn't want to tell her about this adventure before he left because he was afraid she would have talked him out of it. He texted her saying, "I'm fine. Be back shortly." Whew! Sarah just got a text from Luke, and he was ok. *I wonder where he's been all morning.*

When Luke returned, Lynda asked if they both wanted to go shopping, and of course, Luke didn't want to go. He had things on his mind and said he wouldn't be good company. With Christmas a little over a month away, he wanted to plan something for Lynda and Sarah that they'd never forget. The girls left for shopping and fun, and Luke decided to clean up the house the best that he could while they were gone. It was going to be a little surprise for them. As he cleaned, he was trying to come up with some ideas of what he could do for the two of them that would mean something extra special this year. He had all the broken glass picked up and had put all the pictures in a pile. Some were ripped, some weren't, but he didn't want to throw them away. He put the couch back together the best that he could and threw a blanket over it so the cut up cushions were hidden from view. He vacuumed and then headed upstairs to see what he could do up there. Sarah's room was a complete mess! Her mattress was destroyed. He picked some things up but thought he would let Sarah clean it, or that he would help her at least when she was ready.

He decided to go grocery shopping. There was a list started on the fridge, so he grabbed that and made sure he had his credit card. His parents had given it to him a while ago, and he might as well use it. Armed with these items, he left for the store. Walking around the grocery store, he ran into Detective Hastings.

THE KIDNAPPING

"Luke, good to see you. Lynda called me this morning and said you were missing."

"I went up to see my mother and tell her to have Stella leave us alone."

"Oh. How did that go?"

"I didn't have a conversation with her. I just told her that and left."

"I see. Are you here shopping alone?"

"Yes. The girls went shopping so Sarah would have some clothes since they were all destroyed by that maniac."

"Yes, she is something else, isn't she?"

"Yeah, something! Well, I'm going to get this stuff back to Lynda's. Have a nice night, Detective."

"You as well, Luke. Glad to see that you are all right."

"Thanks."

Once he checked out, he headed back to start dinner. He texted Sarah once back at the house to let her know not to eat, that there would be a surprise for them when they returned home.

Sarah told her mom, "Luke said not to eat, that he was planning a surprise."

"Well, that sounds nice, but I'm going out with the detective this evening, remember? He's making me dinner."

"Oh, that's right. Are you excited?"

"I don't know. I'm a little scared and a little excited. I don't know what I'm going to wear, and I don't know how to act. It's been so long since I've been on a date."

Sarah laughed at her mom and said, "You will be just fine! Besides, he wants to go out with you, so don't act any differently than you normally do, and things should go great."

"I sure hope you're right! He seems like a nice man, and I do feel safe with him, so maybe it will be all right."

"Mom, you will be fine, ok? If it doesn't go well, you don't have to go out with him again. Besides, isn't that guy that wanted to look at that house also waiting to find out if you will go out with him?"

"Yes, that's true. I will need to get in touch with him tomorrow to find out when he can go house hunting with me."

"See, Mom, you have options, and I'm happy that you are finally going to date someone! It's been over a year and a half since dad left, and I just want you to be happy again."

"I know it's been a while, but what your dad did blindsided me, and I wasn't ready to put myself out there again. I don't know if I'm ready now, but, I just need to bite the bullet and give it a shot, right?"

"Right!"

26

Once they arrived back at the house, Lynda and Sarah noticed that the house had been cleaned up and they asked Luke about it and he said, "Yeah. I figured it would be nice to come home and have it at least picked up a little bit. I also did the grocery shopping."

Lynda said, "Well, Luke, you didn't have to do that. What do I owe you for the groceries?"

"Absolutely nothing. You letting me stay here is more than payment enough. I just wanted to do something to help out around here, and this was what I came up with."

"And it's a big help too! Thank you very much for being so considerate." With that being said, she went up to get ready for her dinner with Brad. She tried on three different dresses, jeans, and leggings. She called down to Sarah, "Honey, could you come up here for a minute, please?"

"Be right there." Sarah went into mom's room and couldn't believe the mess! "Mom, what happened in here? Was Stella in here too?"

"No," she responded quietly. "I can't find a thing to wear!" Sara laughed.

"Oh, Mom, anything you put on will look fabulous. Just pick something!"

"Aw, thanks, sweetie! I just don't want to be too overdressed or too underdressed. My dilemma is we will be eating dinner at his house, so I think that I can just wear jeans."

"Yes, that's the best plan. A pair of jeans with a dressy top should work out great!"

"Ok. I better hurry up. I'm supposed to be there by seven o'clock. That doesn't leave me a lot of time."

"You'll be fine. A lady can always be fashionably late."

"I am going to be, too, if I don't hurry up. Thanks for your advice."

"No problem. I'm going down to see what Luke's making dinner. He wouldn't let me in the kitchen when we came home, and it smells amazing."

Sarah went back downstairs and into the kitchen. Whatever he was making smelled fantastic. She asked him, "So, what's the big surprise?"

"I can't tell you, it's a surprise."

"You know it's just for me and you, right?"

"Yep, I do."

"Well, aren't you sweet?"

"Yep, I am!" Grinning, he turned from the countertop where he was mixing up a salad and said, "Did I tell you today how pretty you are?"

"No, you haven't," she said walking up to him and putting her arms around his waist and resting her head on his chest. "Well, you are, Sarah Wheeler. Beautiful in fact, and I consider myself a very lucky guy!"

"I'm the lucky one. If I hadn't started tutoring you in algebra, we wouldn't be here right now."

"If my crazy mother and that insane Stella had anything to do with it, neither one of us would be."

"I can't wait until the trials are over and done with! I want to put this behind us and move on. Will you be staying with us over Christmas, or will you be moving back to that house?"

"I'm not sure what is going to happen. I don't know if I can move back in. I'll have to check with the police since it was a crime scene."

"I hope you stay here! It's nice having you here with me. I feel so safe when you're here."

"I like to be here too." He squeezed her a little bit tighter and gave her a kiss. Lynda came down and showed them what she had picked out. They both complimented her choice, and she left.

27

They were all alone. They had been alone before, after school, while she was tutoring him and when he was teaching her to drive, but this time, it just felt different. Luke told her to go sit down so that he could bring dinner to the table for them. He had already set the table, so she went and sat down. He brought over a couple plates for them. He had broiled up some steaks, made twice-baked potatoes and sweetcorn for their dinner. Sarah didn't realize how hungry she was until she got a whiff of what she was about to eat. Her stomach growled hungrily.

"Thank you, Luke, for making dinner! It's been a while since I've seen anything that looked and smelled this good."

"I know. We just need to relax and think only about ourselves this evening."

"I don't have a problem with that. Let's dig in."

They talked about having to go back to school and face the kids there. They already knew it was all around the school because a couple of Luke's friends had texted him to see if he was all right. They couldn't talk to anyone about what happened since it was an ongoing investigation. They were glad because it still blew their minds to think about what she could have done to them.

When they were about halfway through their meal, he said, "I have something to tell you."

"Uh-oh, this doesn't sound good. You're breaking up with me, aren't you? You wanted me to have one last great meal, and now you're dumping me?"

"No, not even close. I went to see my mom today. I told her to have Stella stop all of this insanity and to stop now. I told her enough is enough and that she better make this right."

"Wow. How do you feel after seeing and talking to her again? Are you ok?"

"Yeah, I'm fine. She was ecstatic that I was there for a visit but not about what I had to say. I said what I needed to, and I left."

"That must have been a little bit hard on you."

"Actually, I've been so angry with her for so many years that it felt good, no, great to just tell her something and be able to walk away. What she did to me when I was a kid is fucked up, and I hope that this therapist can help me get over it. I have so much anger toward her!"

"You know what? You were right, tonight we just need to think about ourselves. Do you want to watch a movie after we clean up?"

"No. I have a better idea," he said secretively.

"You don't say? Whatever could it be?"

"You'll see. Let's get the kitchen cleaned up, and I'll show you what else this evening has in store for us." They cleaned up the kitchen, put all the dishes in the dishwasher, and washed up what didn't fit.

"Come with me, please?"

"Where are we going? Do I need a jacket?"

"No, just come with me." She followed him up the stairs where they walked right by her bedroom and went to the room he was staying in. He flipped on the lights, and she gasped.

"Luke, what's this?"

"Well, I know your mattress was destroyed, and I can sleep on the couch until your new one comes. I wanted you to stay here until then, so I fixed it up a little bit for you."

"I love it! That was so sweet of you!"

She looked up at him smiled and standing on her tiptoes, gave him a big kiss. The room was perfect for a few days, and he had tried to make it into her room without moving all of her stuff.

"I'm glad you like it! I just feel so bad. None of this stuff would have ever happened to you if you hadn't met me. My crazy mother wouldn't have kidnapped you and then the man she married wouldn't have taken you with him and Stella wouldn't have kidnapped both of us. It just seems hard to believe that all of this has happened. I don't know how to make any of it up to you, but I will try my hardest to make sure that you know how much I love you."

Knowing how hard this was on him, she thanked him again and said, "You could not have known that any of that was going to happen! Hell, if I had known, I certainly wouldn't have wanted to meet you. I am glad that we are together now, though, and hope to God nothing else happens to either of us." They hugged and kissed and decided to go back downstairs to watch a movie.

It isn't exactly what I had in mind, thought Luke, *but I don't want to rush anything.* Sarah was relieved that they were going down to watch a movie. She had never been with a guy before, and although she thought she wanted to be with Luke, she was terrified. *It's going to happen,* she thought. *I just want to be a little more prepared.* They picked a movie and curled up together on the couch. She had promised her mom that she would talk to Luke about being protected if they had sex, but she didn't want to ruin this moment or anything about this day. Luke was lying there thinking, *This is the life! Girl of my dreams by my side, my parents both in jail, crazy stalker girl in jail, I'm almost eighteen, and it's almost Christmas. Life has sure turned around in the last couple of months!* He was happy, but he wanted to take it to the next level with Sarah. He knew that she was young and inexperienced and that made it all the more exciting. He wanted to be her first and only. *I'd better just keep my hands to myself,* he thought. *I don't need any more problems for us, and I will have her for the rest of my life, so there's no hurry.*

They had both fallen asleep on the couch by the time Lynda came home. After she walked in and saw them sleeping with the TV on, she decided to let them sleep. She would talk to them in the morning. She turned off the TV and went in to get a glass of water and was glad to see that they had cleaned up the kitchen. While walking up the stairs, she replayed her evening in her head for the millionth time.

THE KIDNAPPING

Brad had made them a great dinner of chicken parmesan with garlic bread, a salad, and a bottle of Chianti. They chatted over dinner trying to steer clear of talking about what had been happening lately. They talked about their interests, hobbies, jobs, everything you talk about when you're getting to know someone. There was soft music playing in the living room, and they moved there to continue to get to know one another. They ended up making out, and Lynda enjoyed it but thought it best to leave before something happened that she might not be ready for. She scolded herself now thinking *that might have been just what I needed*. She was lonely and didn't realize it until she had dinner with Brad. He was a great guy, and she really enjoyed his company. He had asked her to go out again next week, and she had agreed. There wasn't anything planned, just that they wanted to see each other again.

As she daydreamed, she thought about Mr. Willis—Charles. He was good-looking, had a boat load of money, and she was going to try to sell him a house. She wasn't sure if she should date him and thought that maybe if she found him a house, they could go out after her job was done. She had not dated a client, and she wasn't going to start now. Besides, she did like Brad, and he made her feel safe. She hadn't ever had a dilemma about dating before. She'd never dated more than one person at a time, and she didn't think that she wanted to start that now. In the morning, she'd call Charles and see when he was free to look at houses. This would give her an idea when she would be able to go out with Brad again. Being a little tired and very relaxed from the wine, Lynda took a shower and got ready for bed. She drifted off to sleep as soon as her head hit the pillow.

28

Once the kids left for school, Lynda called Charles to set up some times with him for house showings. She talked to him for just a few minutes but had several days when they could go house hunting. She made arrangements with the other realtors, had a schedule ready, and called Charles back.

"Sorry to hang up on you so quickly before, Lynda. I was in a meeting."

"Oh, that's no problem at all, Charles. I have Saturday all set up for house hunting. I have four places for us to look all in the Chico area, and they are all in the price range of the other one I was going to show you. I'll send you the MLS listings so that you can tell me if you don't want to go to any of them."

"I'm sure whatever you've picked out will be just fine. After we're done looking at houses, would you like to have dinner with me?"

"Well, Charles, I don't usually date my clients. For now, I'd like to keep business and pleasure apart if that's ok with you."

"I thought you might say that, and I admire your standards! I could fire you, but then you'd be even less likely to go out with me."

"I'm glad you understand. Let's meet at the realtor's office on Saturday and then we can go in one car, if that works for you?"

"That will work just fine, Lynda. Until Saturday."

"Goodbye, Charles. See you then."

Lynda was pleased that he hadn't pressed the issue of dating, and if after spending some time with him, she wasn't attracted to him, she wouldn't have a problem saying no. She didn't know if she liked having two men in her life at the same time.

Her cell rang, and it was Brad. "Hello, Brad" she said warmly. "How are you today?"

"I'm just fine. How are you?"

"I'm great. I have four houses to show a client this Saturday in Chico. Luke cleaned up the house yesterday while we were gone, and the two of them seem to be getting along despite everything that has happened."

"It's nice to hear a smile in your voice. Any chance that we could have that second date this weekend? I was going to see if you wanted to go out Saturday, but you seem to already have plans. What about lunch on Sunday?"

"I think that sounds lovely! Where are we going?"

"You just leave that to me. I'll pick you up at eleven thirty on Sunday."

"That sounds great! What should I wear, casual or dressy?"

"Anything you want. You look great in anything."

"Well, aren't you nice! Thank you! Ok. I'll be ready at eleven thirty on Sunday. See you then."

"Yes, I'm looking forward to it."

"Me too, bye."

29

Luke and Sarah went to school and were each taken out of their first class to talk to the principal. There were no issues, he just wanted to hear what happened and to assure them that Stella would not be allowed back into the school. He wanted to tell them that no one else would bother them with questions, but he knew he couldn't do that. The school had, however, addressed the student body and asked them to please refrain from bothering the two of them as they had to deal with enough stuff as it was and that they wouldn't be able to talk about anything because the investigation was still ongoing. They left his office and continued on with their day. What a day it had been so far. The teachers had all been kind and forgiving when they didn't have their homework done. The kids on the other hand were horrible. Questions were shouted at them all day long. Really awful things being said about Luke's mom and "dad" and that Sarah should just leave him because he was probably just as crazy as they were. How could she let them in her house knowing that his mother was crazy and that he probably didn't fall far from the tree? They knew it was going to be rough, but this was out of control. Thankfully, the day was almost over.

After school, they rode home in silence both thinking about what had transpired throughout the day. Once they walked into the house, they dropped their backpacks and hugged. Sarah started to cry softly.

"Hey, Sarah, what's wrong? Were the kids mean to you? What did they say?"

"Oh, Luke, they were awful but not to me. It's what they said about you and your family. I don't ever want to go back again! I know I have to, but I can't believe how rotten kids can be."

"I know. I heard some pretty awful things today too. I'm so sorry. Again, if you'd never met me, this wouldn't be happening at all. I'm so sorry!"

"It's not your fault, for crying out loud! Why can't people see that? You didn't tell your mom to kidnap me and then have Larry take me out of the state. You didn't tell Stella to be an insane, psycho person and try to hurt me! I just wish people would mind their own business!"

They just stood there hugging until Sarah stopped crying. Her mom came home about twenty minutes later and seeing that Sarah had been crying asked her what was wrong. She and Luke told her about school and how rotten the kids had been.

"That's it. I'll call the principal tomorrow and tell him to make it stop."

"I'm not going to school tomorrow," Sarah exclaimed.

"Me neither."

"Well, I'll call and get homework assignments for both of you for up to a week. You will have to catch up on what you've missed so far and then do that work too."

"That's fine with me," Sarah insisted.

"Me too," agreed Luke.

30

Lynda decided it was time to get the house ready for Christmas. It might be a good one this year. *Sarah has a boyfriend, I'm seeing someone, and we've gotten the insurance money to replace the items that were ruined.* The kids helped her bring up decorations, and they were all decorating when there was a knock at the door. *Well, who could that be?* Lynda wondered. She went to the door and, before opening it, asked who it was.

"It's me, Brad."

She opened the door and said, "Come on in, Brad. What brings you by? Can I get you something?"

"Thanks, but no. I came here to talk to Luke."

"Oh, ok. Luke, the detective wants to talk to you."

Luke looked a little worried but said, "Ok, no problem."

"Grab your coat. We can go for a walk and talk."

"Ok, be right there." He retrieved his coat and went outside with the detective. "So, Detective, what's up? What do you want to see me about?"

"Well, this isn't easy, but your mother and I had a meeting today and she has told me some things and I need to clear this up, so I thought I'd just come and ask you about it."

"Really? What did she have to say?" He was a little bit nervous now, wondering if she would dare to tell about his role in everything that had happened with Sarah. They started to walk down the sidewalk away from the house.

"There is no easy way to say this but did you ask your mom to kidnap Sarah and put her in that fallout shelter? She told me everything that happened, and I need to know if she is lying to us, or if you are lying."

"That bitch! Why in the world would I want to kidnap Sarah or have someone kidnap her?"

"Because you wanted to be her knight in shining armor."

"Look, I love Sarah, and I have since I met her. I wouldn't do anything to hurt her."

"You didn't do anything, your mother did. The way she tells it, you wanted Sarah to be held until you could save her. You didn't count on Larry coming around and taking her with him on one of his little trips. Why would you do it? Don't you think that was taking things a little bit too far? She doesn't think that you had anything to do with it now, but she did, and she was right. You've been stalking her practically since you moved to town. Why? What is it about her that you wanted to see her kidnapped and put through such torture?"

"There wasn't any torture! I was going to come home from school, and later on that night, I was going to go down there and find her. When I went down there, and she was gone, I couldn't believe it. I was already mad at my mother for not doing things the way that I wanted them and for telling that stupid bitch Stella that I liked her. That messed things up more than anything else and then when we found out that Larry took her with him, I could have killed my mom. I only wanted to be Sarah's hero! I love her and want to protect her for the rest of our lives. You can't say anything to her! I'll kill you if you do."

"Now look, son, don't you threaten me, I'm no school girl. You can make this easy on yourself, or you can make it difficult, that's up to you. You should go back in that house and tell them both the truth."

"No, I won't! I'll take this secret to my grave."

"It's not a secret any longer. I'm going to have to arrest you for conspiring to commit a kidnapping."

"*No!*"

Luke took off down the sidewalk running as fast as he could. Brad ran back to his squad car and jumped in chasing after Luke. Luke's mind was racing, *he can't tell her. She can't find out. She loves me, and if she finds out, she'll hate me! I'm going to find a way to be with her, but first, I need to get away.* He ran out toward the orchards on the south side of town. The detective saw him heading in that direction and radioed dispatch to send all available units toward the orchards. Brad thought, *he can't go up into the mountains, he doesn't have warm enough clothes on.* Luke finally stopped running. He couldn't run any farther. He was out of breath. He hid in the orchard the best that he could. He knew he couldn't go into the mountains and hoped he could hide out here until dark when he could then try to get back to his house and hide out there. There were very few places to hide. It was acres and acres of trees, and he was surprised that he hadn't seen or heard the cops yet. Maybe he gave them the slip and could start heading back to his house.

Dark was approaching, and Brad was unsure where Luke was hiding. The other officers were driving slowly around the orchard trying to locate Luke. Brad decided to call out to Luke in hopes that he was close enough for him to hear. He said into the bull horn, "Luke! This is Detective Hastings. Come out with your hands up. Do it, son, things will be easier if you do. Luke, I'm trying to help you out. Things are going to get very difficult for you if you continue to hide. If you come out now, I will tell them that you cooperated with me, and they might go a little easier on you. Come on out."

"Ok. I'm coming out. Don't shoot." Luke revealed himself from his hiding spot and saw that Hastings was very close to where he had been hiding.

"Turn around and lace your fingers behind your head," he instructed. Brad read him his rights and put him in the squad car. He then radioed the others to let them know that he had apprehended the suspect and was bringing him to jail. "Do you have anything you'd like to say before I bring you in and book you?"

"Is there any way that this doesn't get back to Sarah?"

"I'm sorry, Luke, she will find out about it and sooner than you think. When you don't go back to the house, she's going to wonder why and then she will find out. I'm afraid that this little scheme of yours didn't work out quite the way you wanted it to."

"It didn't work out at all the way I wanted it to. Why would my mother tell you? I don't understand. She did some really disgusting things to me as a child and said that she would help me with this, and I told her that I wouldn't mention those things again."

"Lynda told me about what your mother did, and I'm very sorry that you've had to go through so much turmoil; however, it doesn't change what you've done, and it also doesn't give you an excuse. If you love someone, you have to let them make their own choices. You can't make them love you."

"She does love me though. I'll never find anyone like her again."

"Son, where you're going, you won't need to worry about that for a while. You're looking at a number of very serious charges. I hope that while you're in there, you can get some serious help for yourself. You still need to let go of what happened to you as a boy."

"I don't need anything except Sarah!" he said vehemently.

"I don't believe that will ever happen now. You've made some incredibly poor choices, and now I will have to go over to the house to let them both know what happened to you."

"Will you please tell her that I love her, and I am so very sorry for everything?"

"I really don't think that's a good idea," he said as they pulled up to the jail. "You'll be booked into the system and then allowed your one phone call. Do your parents have a lawyer? I would suggest you use that call to find someone to defend you."

"I'll call Sarah and tell her I love her myself."

"Wouldn't you rather try to reach someone that might be able to help you get out of trouble instead of wasting your call on someone that will never have anything to do with you again? Your parents' trials are going to be starting soon, and they just might put you on trial with them. Stella's trial will probably start around the same time as well. Since they are related offenses, and it was against the same person, I could see them trying you all at the same time."

That wasn't exactly the news that Luke wanted to hear, but he would face the music and deal with things one day at a time. He had hoped that he would have been able to tell Sarah about this sometime down the road but that won't happen now.

After being booked, Luke gave up all of his possessions, changed into jail clothes, and was placed in a cell until it was time for his trial. Brad put all of his belongings in a bag, labeled and dated it and it would be stored until Luke was out of jail. Brad headed back over to Lynda's house to break the news to them. When he finished telling them what he knew, Sarah started to cry and then she got angry. *I'll never let anyone do this to me again,* she thought! *How dare he think that he could plan my kidnapping and still want me to be with him and love him! I hate him! This will be the last time that anyone does anything to hurt me again!* All of them could rot in prison for all she cared. She excused herself, went upstairs, flung herself on the bed, and cried. She reached for her phone and deleted his number and every picture that they had ever taken. She wanted to erase him from her memory! She lay down on her bed, started to cry all over again, and vowed that this will be the last time that she would be a victim.

The district attorney decided to try the four of them together since all the crimes involved the same young woman. Sarah sat through that first day, and it made her so angry and hurt. She sat there steely eyed and stoic while she listened to the happenings of the trial. When it came time for her turn on the stand, she told everything that she could remember about the day that Julia and Larry kidnapped her. She recounted everything that had happened with Luke and their kidnapping. She had thought she was so lucky to have him, how she had fallen in love with him, and now couldn't even look at him. Relieved when she was told she could step down, she walked right out of the courtroom. She'd come back tomorrow, maybe. She was one of the last few to testify. Several days later, the trial was over. Larry got charged for kidnapping a minor, transporting her over state lines, and drugging her twice (which is considered a form of torture). The charges were considered felonies, and he received twelve years, which was the max he could receive. Since Julia had been the one who had actually done the kidnapping, she was charged the maximum of four years for that felony. Luke was charged with two counts of kidnapping, conspiracy to commit kidnapping, and fleeing and threatening a peace officer for which he received a maximum sentence of fourteen years and would forever be labeled a felon at the age of eighteen. Stella received nine years for two counts of kidnapping and brandishing a weapon. Since all four of them had been charged with felonies, they were all going to prison. Sarah was relieved when the sentencing hearings were over. Knowing they were all going away to prison gave her great satisfaction. She swore to herself that she would do her damndest to help victims like her when she got older.

31

Sarah went back to school about a week before Christmas break was to start. Everyone was looking at her, pointing, and talking about her. Sarah decided she'd had enough, and it was time to address the student body. She asked the principal if she could make an announcement over the PA system to explain to them what had happened to her. He told her he thought that would be a good idea so that everyone could move on. The next morning when she got to school, she addressed the whole school explaining what had happened. When she finished her account of what happened, she headed back to class holding her head high and walking through the halls like the last few months hadn't been the most terrifying and awful months of her whole life. She'd finish out the school year here and talk to her mom about switching schools. She would be getting her license soon, and Chico wasn't that far away. She could drive to school over there.

Brad came over one evening for dinner and asked Sarah, "How is everything going? Kids treating you ok?"

"Everything is fine. I addressed the student body and explained what happened to me. No one has really talked to me since I did that. At least I don't hear them talking about me anymore."

"I understand 100%."

"So do I, but honey, you've got to talk about what's happened. You need an outlet. Would you like to talk to a counselor at school or a therapist?"

"No, Mom, I don't. I don't need to talk about it. I've talked about it, I've listened to it, and I lived it. I don't need to rehash it any more. What I do need is for people to leave me the hell alone and for my life to get back to normal. I'm not sure if that will ever happen, but that's what I need."

"Ok. I won't push you, but I'm here if you change your mind."

"Thanks, Mom. I'm sorry for snapping, I just want my life to be normal again. I was thinking about something too. Since I'll be getting my driver's license before the next school year, is it ok if I go to Chico and finish out school there? No one knows me there, and it would kind of be a fresh start for me."

"We'll talk about it when it gets closer, but that might not be a bad idea."

"Cool, thanks, Mom!" She excused herself from the table and went up to her room.

"I have some news about that dead man they found in that house that you were trying to sell." Brad said after Sarah went upstairs.

"Oh? I almost forgot about that poor man. Who was he? What was he doing there?"

"Obviously, he was from out of town, and the car was registered to his fiancé that's why they thought it might have been stolen. After the autopsy, they discovered that he was filled with cancer, and it seems that he went there to die. They reached out his fiancée, and she said that he had found out about the cancer a couple of weeks ago. He disappeared with her car and ended up in that house. She told the Chico police that he had grown up in that house and must have decided to die there. They estimate that he was dead for a few days before he was found."

"Well, at least he wasn't killed and then put there. Have the owners been told this? They may want to put the house back on the market again. Of course, they'll have to spend some money and have it cleaned. Thank you for telling me. I was curious to know what happened."

"I think the Chico police have called the owners and told them what happened, and I'm pretty sure if they wanted to sell it before, they'll want to sell it now."

"I'll give them a call in the morning, but all I want to do right now is just be here with you."

"That sounds like a plan I can get behind."

They went to the living room and watched some TV and then headed up to bed about midnight. Brad had been a regular visitor because Lynda told him she wouldn't leave Sarah home alone for any length of time. Lynda stopped by Sarah's door before heading to her own room and thought she heard her crying. She opened the door softly and saw that she was fast asleep. *Thank goodness*, she thought. *My poor girl has been through so much. Maybe a different school for two years wouldn't be such a bad idea.*

32

Sarah was up early the next day making breakfast when her mom walked into the kitchen saying, "Morning, kiddo. What smells so good? I'm famished."

"Waffles and bacon. I thought it would be nice to have breakfast for you and Brad, just to thank you both for what you've already done for me and what you continue to do. All of my schoolwork is caught up, and I'm even thinking about going to summer school to get a jump on graduation. I'm not taking what happened to me lightly. I'm going to do something about it. I won't be a victim again."

"Brad has already left. Good for you, sweetheart! What are you thinking about taking in summer school?"

"I want to finish whatever mandatory classes I can so that I can concentrate on starting college early. I want to get into law enforcement and be a detective like Brad."

"What? Are you serious? I don't really like that idea at all."

"Well, of course not. I'm your little girl, and you don't want anything else to happen to me. But for me, I feel like a totally different person. I'm not scared anymore. I realized the other day when I talked about what happened to the whole school that there might be one person out there that I helped. I *want* to help people through situations like this. If it wasn't for Brad always being there for us, I don't know that I would have believed in the system. He is such a great guy and seems like he is always in the thick of things, and I want to be that someone to some poor family that might go through the same thing. I'm not naïve enough to think this will never happen again. If it can happen in a little town like Paradise, it can happen anywhere."

"I see that you've been giving this some thought."

"I have, and I'm finally excited for what my future holds, not scared."

"We might have to check on you getting into college early, but I think you've got a great plan. I don't have to like what you want to do with your future, but I *will* support you 100% in anything that you choose even if it means sleepless nights, frantic phone calls, and all that goes along with it."

"Oh Mom" she laughed, "you make it sound like I'm going to war."

"Essentially, you will be. The war on crime."

"I'm going to be a special detective though. I want to only work with kidnapping victims. I know exactly what they are going through, and I know that I can help them."

Lynda reached across the table and squeezed Sarah's hand and said, "I *know* you will, sweetie."

After breakfast was finished and cleaned up, Lynda decided to call the owners of the property in Chico to see if they wanted to put it back on the market. They decided that since the man hadn't been killed there that they could indeed put it back on the market. *Great,* Lynda thought. *I know just the person that wants to buy it.* She called Charles to see if he still wanted to look at the house since the owners would be putting it back on the market. He said he would like that very much. They decided to meet at 2:00 p.m. While she drove out there, she had this sense of déjà vu and didn't like it one bit. She called Sarah to make sure she was ok and when she heard her voice, thought she was just being silly. She got to the house, and there was no car in the driveway this time which relieved her. *So far so good,* she thought. Charles pulled up before she got the key in the door, and she waited for him outside.

"I don't know what it looks like in here or even how it smells, they just told me today to relist it, and I thought you'd like to see it right away."

THE KIDNAPPING

"Yes, thank you for that. I've wanted to see it since the first day we were here and that may be why I haven't settled for any of the other lovely houses you've shown me."

"Shall we?" She unlocked the door and pushed it open. While it didn't smell as badly as she thought it should, it didn't smell the best. "I thought it would be worse." She laughed.

"Honestly, so did I." He smiled at her. They toured the house and it was exactly the house he had been looking for and the one he wanted. He was very happy that he waited to see this one before buying another one. "*Sold!*" he exclaimed.

"Really? Oh, Charles, I'm so happy for you."

"Thank you, Lynda, for sticking with me through this process until I found the right place."

"This one will have to be deep cleaned before you move in, and I'll talk to the owners about getting it done quickly."

"Don't bother. I can have it done before I move in. Of course, I'll have to schedule an inspection, but I don't think they'll tell me anything about this place that would make me not want to buy it. Not even a dead body could stop me, obviously." He was positively on cloud nine.

"Well, ok. if that's what you want. I do have paperwork with me if you'd like to write up an offer. I can send it to them today."

"I'd like that. Let's go get some coffee and fill out the paperwork."

"That sounds like a great idea."

She was thrilled this was finally over! Charles bought the house, and she was going to make a pretty penny on this sale. Hell, she would make enough to send Sarah to college. This was one of the best days in a really, really long time, and she couldn't wait to get home to tell Sarah. Once the paperwork was completed, Lynda called the owners to let them know that she had sold their property. They were astounded!

"We'll recommend you to all of our friends that sell in the area. You get results and quickly too!"

"Oh, that would mean a great deal to me. Thank you so much." Everything was looking up.

33

That evening when she returned home, she came in with her arms loaded with stuff. "Sarah? Honey, come down here. I need some help!"

"Be right there, Mom." She hurried down the stairs to see what her mom needed. Her eyes got huge, and she looked at her mom. "What is all of this? Did you rob a store?"

"No, silly. I sold that house in Chico to Charles."

"Mom, that's fantastic! Congratulations! We should celebrate!"

"What do you think I've been doing?"

They both laughed. It felt so good to have the stress of everything behind them finally. Everything was unloaded from the car, presents were put under the tree, and other things put away.

Sarah asked, "What's going to happen with you and Brad? You guys seem to be getting close, and he stays here a lot."

"I'm not sure, honey. I really like him a lot, and I like having him here. What do you think?"

"Do you trust him?"

"With our lives. Why?"

"Just making sure."

"What's with the questions? Did something happen that I should know about?"

"No. I'm just making sure that you're happy, that's all. Changing the subject, are we going to move? We could move to Chico now. With the commissions that you just made, we could buy a house there and sell this one."

"I was thinking that we might move but not necessarily to Chico. It wouldn't matter much where we live, but I do want to get out of this house, it has so many ghosts now."

"It sure does. I think we should look into something there. It would be closer to a new high school for me." Just then, there was a knock at the door.

Lynda said, "I wonder who that could be?" She went to the door and asked, "Who is it?"

"It's me, Brad." She swung open the door and grabbed him and gave him a big wet kiss.

"Well, to what do I owe that greeting?"

"To the fact that I sold that house in Chico to Charles today, and I just made a boat load of money!"

"That's terrific, Lynda! I knew you could do it. It was just a matter of time."

They went into the living room where he and Sarah said hello. Sarah excused herself, grinned at Brad, and went upstairs.

"What was that all about?" Lynda asked curiously.

"I don't know what you're talking about."

"That look she just gave you. What's going on?"

"I have something I've been thinking about for a while now, and I want to get your take on it," he said as he got down on one knee and presented her with a diamond ring that looked it cost a year's salary. "Lynda Wheeler, will you marry me? I love you and want to spend the rest of my life with you and Sarah if you ladies will have me."

"Will I marry you? Um, you've taken me by surprise. I'll have to think about it, and we have to ask Sarah."

"I already said yes!" she shouted from upstairs. They both started to laugh, and Lynda said, "Yes! Yes! Yes!"

"You've made me the happiest man in all of Paradise!"

He stood, pulling her into his arms, and she exclaimed, "And you've made me the happiest woman in all of Paradise!"

Sarah was already down the stairs, joined in the hug, and said, "*Now* can we move to Chico?" They all laughed and Lynda and Sarah shared a thought: *This was going to be the best Christmas ever!*

About the Author

Mary lives in northern Minnesota and enjoys reading, gardening, cooking, fishing, crocheting, and writing. She enjoys time spent with family and friends and loves to snuggle and play with her dog. She enjoys new experiences with the ones she loves. She believes that no matter your age, never stop hoping and dreaming because then you'll have nothing to aspire to. If you have nothing to aspire to, you stop living.

CPSIA information can be obtained
at www.ICGtesting.com
Printed in the USA
FSHW011303071021
85314FS